Giants of Contem

CW00458769

Series Editor
Omnia Amin

This book series targets the publication of well-known names in modern and contemporary Arab literature, including feminist writer Dr. Nawal El Saadawi and renowned poets Mahmoud Darwish and Ahmed Hijazi, as well as potential young writers and winners of the Arab Booker Prize. The aim of this series is to introduce to English-speaking readers new material and important works from the canon of Arab literature that already enjoy an established audience and are seen as landmarks in the Arab literary tradition. Books in this series will also introduce rising stars in contemporary Arab literature whose works are promising and expected to be the landmarks of the future.

More information about this series at
http://www.springer.com/series/15085

Nawal El Saadawi

Diary of a Child Called Souad

Introduced and translated from Arabic
by Omnia Amin

Nawal El Saadawi
Cairo, Egypt

Translated by Omnia Amin

Giants of Contemporary Arab Literature
ISBN 978-1-137-58936-1   ISBN 978-1-137-58730-5 (eBook)
DOI 10.1007/978-1-137-58730-5

Library of Congress Control Number: 2015035296

Translation from the Arabic language edition: *Mothakarat Tifla Ismaha Souad* by Nawal El Saadawi, © Al Saqi 2015. All Rights Reserved.

Cover illustration © Pedro Antonio Salaverría Calahorra / Alamy Stock Photo

Printed on acid-free paper

This Palgrave Macmillan imprint is published by Springer Nature
The registered company is Nature America Inc. New York

ACKNOWLEDGMENTS

Special thanks to Dr. David Palfreyman for his revisions and editing of this project.

CONTENTS

CHAPTER 1

Introduction: Why is Nawal El Saadawi Banned?

THE MAKING OF A LEGEND

It was in 2002 when I first saw Dr. Nawal El Saadawi give a talk on comparative literature at a conference held at Cairo University. I was already familiar with El Saadawi's writing through a number of novels and works of nonfiction that I had read and studied. I had always wondered why she is feared so much in some quarters, to the extent that her writing and talks are banned. On this occasion she spoke about creativity and courage, and I will never forget the sparkle in her eyes that continued throughout the talk despite the sneering and hissing of a mostly hostile and disapproving audience. I saw a simply dressed woman with the famous black and white Palestinian shawl around her neck, which in itself indicated her sympathy for the Palestinian cause and made a political statement. The first

© Omnia Amin 2016, Published by Palgrave Macmillan, 1
A Division of Nature America Inc.
N. El Saadawi, *Diary of a Child Called Souad*,
DOI 10.1007/978-1-137-58730-5

thing she said to her audience, which mainly comprised university professors and students, was: *What are you doing in here? Why aren't you outside demonstrating? When we were your age we were out there asking for our rights. We were very different from what you are today.* In fact, on our way into the hall, there was a long queue of students standing for hours on end in the scorching sun in front of a small, closed wooden window waiting for books to be dispensed to them. The scene was not lost on El Saadawi, who looked at the students in amazement and said: *Why are you accepting such humiliation? Why don't you protest and insist on your right to dignified treatment?* Perhaps her remarks fell on deaf ears, but the level of mixed passions she stirred in them made me realize that I was in front of a person worthy of the legend that surrounds her.

This talk was, in fact, the first talk she was ever allowed to give not only in her home country of Egypt but also in the whole of the Arab world. She later confessed to me that she has never been honored by a single university or institute in any Arab country, whereas the rest of the world vies to have her as an honorary professor or a visiting guest of honor.

In the aforementioned talk and in every talk I attended by El Saadawi after that, I realized that her technique is simple but powerful. First, she arouses the passion and emotions of her audience to shock them out of the mundane level of thinking and seeing things. Second, she stretches their imagination to allow them to remove the veil from their eyes and accommodate new possibilities. To achieve this, she starts by using extremely provocative sentences. At this conference she spoke about the connection between creativity and courage, and the gist of her talk was that the act of writing is an act of supreme courage because, to reach the truth, one has to have the courage to go beyond and surpass the limitations and intimidations forced on one by the environment. El Saadawi, in this talk, stated that she was 71 years old; today, a decade after first meeting her, I can see this same fiery spirit and ability to provoke in the first piece of writing she attempted in her early teens. *Diary of a Child Called Souad* was written as a school assignment; it was deemed inappropriate by her teacher, she received a zero grade, and she was told off and asked to rewrite the whole exercise. In other words, Nawal El Saadawi's first piece of extended writing was banned. On reading the book, I soon discovered that the legend that was later to become Nawal El Saadawi is already there. The story of Souad is a courageous creative endeavor by the young El Saadawi to examine the double standards of her surroundings and critique not only her society but also herself. This young girl had the strength and vision to expose the hypocrisy of her own background and form the early budding of what she has become today. *Diary of a Child Called Souad* is, in fact, El Saadawi's first step on a long and arduous journey to show that the act of writing is an act of fighting oppression on personal, social, and political levels. The young Souad understood this, and the Nawal El Saadawi of today is a testimonial to it. By looking at her life and works, especially this first piece of writing, I address in this introduction one question: Why is Nawal El Saadawi considered so dangerous that she has to be banned?

WRITING IS A HISTORY OF OPPRESSION

In her book *Memoirs from the Women's Prison*, El Saadawi speaks for all of the women prisoners jailed with her, not for any crime, but for their thoughts and writing. She says in defiance of the prison authorities:

> *We will not die, and if we are to die we won't die silently, we won't go off in the night without a row, we must rage and rage, we must beat the ground and make it shudder. We won't die without a revolution! (1986: 36)*

The banning of a book or a talk by Nawal El Saadawi becomes more understandable once viewed through the history of her writing, which is a history of oppression brought about by her outspokenness and her sharp confrontations with various authorities. One pauses to ask: What is so threatening in her writing to infuriate churches and mosques and to cause a government to ban a novel? What is so blasphemous in Nawal El Saadawi's writing or talks to cause religious orders and groups to call for her death, first in 1988 and then a second time in 1992? How could telling a story and unfolding a plot create such upheaval against one individual? Could the power of the word be so mighty that presidential election commissions feel threatened and religious orders feel insecure?

Her book *The Novel* was banned all over the Arab world the same year it was released in Arabic in 2005. This was not the first time that El Saadawi's writings or declarations led to such violent actions being taken against her. In 2004, her book *The Fall of the Imam* was also banned; in 1980, following her activism toward bettering the lives of women and her efforts to empower women by bringing together their efforts in a woman's organization, she was thrown in prison at the end of the late President Sadat's regime. What is this one woman capable of that distinguishes her from other feminists and public speakers and writers? More than any other writer in the modern age, El Saadawi has had a profound impact on the lives of men and women by shaping and opening their field of vision. Her books cover a range of topics, from women's oppression in its various forms, to the mutilation of women's bodies through circumcision, to other forms of oppression found in the culture, to the interpretation of religion regarding women's duties, responsibilities, and rights. She is most famous for her critique of "veiling of the mind," which has become synonymous with her name and has inspired the efforts of the Arab Women Solidarity Association (AWSA) that she established and has headed since 1982. She also writes about cultural identity and the threats of a fast-moving globalization process that threatens the mind and the spirit of the rising generations. Her books create an awareness of this imminent threat that deliberately misleads us in the name of freedom and democracy. In her attack El Saadawi spares no one, from the Presidents of superpowers to minor journalists with misdirected and defeatist attitudes. Her arguments respond to a history of suppression that targets not only women but also the whole of humanity to serve the interests of the elite. In her uncovering of the strategies aimed at indoctrinating the citizens of the world, El Saadawi traces historical roots and movements dating from the times of the Pharaohs and ancient civilizations and from the rise of religious institutions and epochal political movements to current events that are the end result of policies deeply set and established in the bone and marrow of our historical heritage. She ties all of this to the rise of women's organizations that resist inequality of every sort, poverty and fundamentalism, and seek to liberate the minds and spirits of both men and women. Calling for the consolidation of women's efforts under global organizations has been regarded as the most threatening of El Saadawi's endeavors, and she has had more than one organization repeatedly closed down.

Her life has set an example of the spirit of continuation. Despite attempts to thwart her efforts by discontinuing her services and closing down her organizations, as well as banning her books, her writing, and even her public speeches and declarations, this woman keeps rising like a phoenix from the flames. She calls for a revolution of the mind, a revolution in rereading and reinterpreting religious dogma and political and social laws and regulations that enslave the individual in the name of the sacred and in the name of democracy.

The simplicity of her background is what makes her a role model for every individual, whether rich or poor, male or female. This is what makes her so threatening. Authorities fear the stubbornness of her spirit, her faith in her own efforts, and the success of her achievements. Her character moves every individual in word and flesh in a world that lacks a proper political figure or leader who commands a mass following. When she started out as a young female doctor in Egypt in the 1950s, she went against all that was considered taboo or sacred. Even her family life is testimony that she becomes what she advocates. Dr. Sherif Hetata, her ex-husband and companion for the majority of her life, a writer, and an ardent supporter of her efforts, has shown his belief in what El Saadawi is achieving. Also, her children serve as examples of spirits that have grown to be free thinkers. Her daughter, Dr. Mona Helmy, who is also a writer and a poet and has a weekly column in *Tahrir Daily*, created outrage with her declaration that she wants to change her name to include her mother's name in addition to her father's. As a result, they were both summoned to court and accused of apostasy, but they were later cleared. Mona's efforts won for every Egyptian child born outside marriage the right to carry the mother's name. Her son, Atef Hetata, is a renowned film director, which shows that the whole family displays a spirit nurtured to create and invent. They have endorsed as a family the belief in equality and the freedom to act and speak what they believe to be true and intrinsic to the rise of human values and the liberation of the human spirit.

Her danger lies in her own self, because she embodies the revolution she calls for. *Diary of a Child Called Souad*, written by El Saadawi when she was a child, is a testimonial to this fact. As a child, she instinctively exposed the hypocritical socio-religious and educational construct around her. She uncovers women's silence and lack of representation as she looks at and describes her grandmother who lives in the shadow of her grandfather:

> *As for her grandmother, she is silent all the time. She sits with her full, pale body wrapped in a black silk dress. Her thick, pale legs are covered by transparent black stockings. She has a round, pale face and her complexion is sagging but she has no wrinkles. Her eyes are unlike other people's eyes. She does not have any black or white in them but all one color: grey. They look as if they have never seen the light or the sun, or as if their black has melted into their white from lots of crying or lots of sleep. Her plump, pale hands rest in her lap. They are small but sagging from waiting for a time longer than time itself.*

A similar description is used years later in El Saadawi's autobiography, *My Papers...My Life*, when she again describes her grandmother. She exposes the oppressed life she led and narrates how when her grandmother is finally released by the death of her husband, she does not get to enjoy her freedom because she develops cancer and dies.

In El Saadawi's later novels, the characters described by the young Souad are developed into more complex figures, like Miriam the poet in *The Novel*, another surrogate of El Saadawi, who declares in her poetry:

> *Freedom is knowledge,*
> *It is the motive power behind everything,*
> *Even behind poetry and novels!*
> *Why else*
> *is the gun in prison more innocent*
> *than pen and paper? (2009: 190)*

The influence of El Saadawi's pen and paper has reached beyond the range of any weapon as she penetrates the minds of her readers. The history of her writing proves that to write the truth and to live with courage is to confront a history of oppression. Her ability to withstand all the attacks from religious and governmental institutions is what makes her the most threatening woman of our time.

THE MOST WANTED WOMAN

El Saadawi poses a threat on different levels. The first is on the level of writer of fiction and nonfiction alike. Being a physician by profession, she has spoken freely about women's bodies and problems with a voice of informed authority and not as just another woman who feels injustice and wants to release her anger against society and her female condition. The second level is that of a public speaker and lecturer who speaks directly to her audience in a provocative way. Her manner arouses indignation, and people are quick to take offense as she tries to tear the veil from their eyes. She refuses to allow her audience to hold onto their comfort zones, because she believes that change can only take place if there is courage to question what we think is of unshakable value. It manifests in her exposure of limiting ideas and the corruption of the system of political economics that wants to make humans slaves of production and mere consumers of the things they produce while posing as a global movement of globalization, economic freedom, and democracy. The third level is that of her activities as head of women's organizations to consolidate women's efforts on a huge scale to fight tyranny of all sorts combined with her efforts to stand for the presidency of Egypt to defy an ongoing political farce in that one president was nominated for life. The fourth level is her private life and personality, much of which is revealed in her autobiographies and in this *Diary of a Child Called Souad*, because Souad is none other than her own voice as a young girl in school. All these factors make El Saadawi a living icon that kindles the spirits of generations. The evolution of her life, from a simple background to becoming the star of the modern intellectual world's fight for human rights and justice, speaks for itself. On all these levels, El Saadawi has one demand. It is the demand of freedom, for which the young Souad's

soul and spirit long, even as she is weighed down
by a socio-political and religious heritage that poses
unanswered questions. She looks at the world
around her and feels lost:

> *Souad closes her lips in silence, trying to gulp down
> the feeling of fear coming from deep inside her. The
> world around her seems awful and mysterious and
> full of enemies: English, Germans, ghosts, thieves
> and djinns that come out from the heart of the sea.
> The sky too appears dreadful and mysterious. Her
> eyes fail to reach its depth and her mind is unable
> to imagine God. How could He sit or sleep in the sky
> and remain suspended like this in the air all night
> and day? What happens if a German plane crashes
> into God in the sky? Or if one of the bombs explodes
> in the atmosphere and burns God? Will God die? If
> He dies will she continue to pray and go to school?
> Or will Doomsday come and all people die including
> pupils and teachers and there will no longer be school,
> classes, exams, failing or anything?*

El Saadawi's message is to free humanity from its
chronic bonds. She is not calling for acts of terror-
ism; she is calling for acts of liberation, not by force
of arms but through the use of the mind. What,
then, is so threatening in her message to arouse
this outrage against her works and person? Hers is
a stirring story of one woman proving herself by
defying her cultural, religious, and historical restrictions and interpretations, the economic subordination of women and broader gender inequality,
female mutilation, political injustice, and the loss of

human rights and dignity. In short, she defies the whole world and spares no one. What makes her so special and so dangerous is her ability to liberate the minds of others because she has managed to liberate herself.

LIBERATION OF/FROM THE MIND

Liberation of the mind is considered an evil. Liberate the mind, tear the veils from it, and you have liberated both the body and the soul; there is no stopping or hindering that liberated person. Our mental inhibitions are our undoing, and El Saadawi has torn the veil equally from the sacred and the profane, the just and the unjust, the human and the divine, the word and the deed, male and female, the corporal and the ethereal, the local and the international, and the inherited and the new. She has catalyzed the integration of a belief system, with a belief in the liberated self by erasing the aforementioned boundaries. She has proven that beliefs can be created and dissolved. They are created by the controlling and ruling classes and dissolved by the power of the mind to tear off those veils. Her words have dissolved with ease the game of right and wrong. The historical games of taboo and limitation have been uncovered in El Saadawi's fiction and nonfiction, in her writing, and in her living example. She has designed a tool to liberate the masses from the dominating global mind that acts like a Big Brother in the modern age. What she is calling for is co-creation of a new space that will unfold into true freedom and creativity for the entire world.

She has achieved this in two different ways: in the role of a message bearer, which she presents in her words and writing, and in the role of a teacher-model, which she embodies in her person. In her *Autobiography Part III*, she says:

> *In my depths lies a yearning for knowledge since childhood. My desire for knowledge was greater than my sexual desire. Overtly masculine, virile men do not attract me. Many men passed through my life. They were attracted to my false femininity, to the luster in my eyes. They thought it was sexual lust. They did not realize that it is the lust for knowledge. They thought I returned their love but soon the tragedy unfolds: traditional masculinity collides with a different form of femininity that does not submit to penetration. (2001: 219)*

What she has written in her autobiography is echoed in her fiction. In El Saadawi's novels, all tenses mingle: past, present, and future. All places, the east and the west, and events mix and unite. All characters, male, female, writers, poets, rich, poor, the ignorant, the thinkers, the educated elite, and the working classes, meet and intermingle. They are all enmeshed together as their stories intersect and dissect each other's lives. They become the mirror image of one another's lives and the expository mirrors that uncover the falsity of the inside. *Diary of a Child Called Souad* is a testimonial to this. The book was written in 1944,

when El Saadawi herself was but a child. What was
intended to be a school homework assignment
turned out to be one of the most valuable and
penetrating books written by the young Nawal,
because it exposes the potential realized by the
older Nawal. Even in those early years we can witness where the danger of her writing and character lie. Young as she was, she simply and naturally
possessed the ability to penetrate the fictional
with nonfiction. As she writes her own autobiography and ascribes it to a girl called Souad, the
border of self and other is dissolved. She shows
the story of three generations of women under
masculine subordination, herself, her mother, and
her grandmother, as Souad listens to her mother's
advice:

> *Your interest, my daughter, is at school and in
> education. Education raises a human being to the
> highest position and I used to love education when
> I was like you. I wished to learn everything: English,
> French, playing the piano and horse-riding. But your
> late grandfather was a tough man. He used to edu-
> cate a girl until the age of fifteen then take her out
> of school and make her stay at home until a bride-
> groom came for her. I cried when he took me out of
> school. I used to hate the house and couldn't stand to
> live in it, especially when my father was in the house.
> He never used to stop quarreling with my mother
> and when he went out I would be happy. When he
> returned I would go into my room and not come out.
> I used to pray that I would marry anyone and leave
> that house. I was sixteen when your father came to
> ask for my hand.*

El Saadawi's novels show that the typical plot in postmodernist literature that speaks of freedom of gender and creative expression is still in need of liberation. The nature of the plot cannot advance if the veiling of the mind continues behind modern petitions for creative expression, freedom, and liberation of the mind and spirit. In her diary, the young Souad has touched on all of this. Souad is an example of how the personal turns into the political. In *Diary of a Child Called Souad*, we see the oppression of all the female characters in one way or another. We witness her grandfather's dominance over the household and her grandmother's and aunt's silent voices. We also see how Souad herself grows to join the long lineage of silent females:

> *She no longer asks herself many old questions from childhood. She realizes that questioning is forbidden and such thinking is a form of disbelieving in God and in God's justice. God is just, whether He is fair, unjust or oppressive; and God is merciful whether He slaughters children or does not slaughter them.*

The individual and personal struggles of the characters are not divorced from the political arena or the public community as characters re-enact what is happening politically in their private lives. The political scene in El Saadawi's fiction is gripped by scandals, hypocrisy, and falsity. For example, Rustum in *The Novel* is the character who embodies all the political patriarchal corruption and who is ironically a writer and speaks of possibilities of liberation and democracy. Through this character, El Saadawi evidently attacks the current political national and international figureheads. Just before Rustum's death, the young woman looks at him and sees that he is decaying, that his authority is losing its hold:

> Rustum's face seems to her long and pale, as if he were at the end of his life. His nose has become bigger relative to the rest of his features. It is longer, more pointed and beak like. His eyes are grey and bewildered. The hair of his thick eyebrows is falling out, along with the hair at the front of his head. His forehead has become higher than it used to be. It comprises half his skull, like the skull of a president or a great writer or a member of Al Shura Council or the Parliament. The flesh on his neck droops and the veins protrude under his double chin. He almost resembles George Bush the father, or the son, or the Holy Ghost.

In the last sentence, El Saadawi deals a blow to all institutions, whether they are cultural, political, or religious. The same decay is echoed in other novels by El Saadawi in the romantic and social relationships among the characters who continuously exchange roles and lovers, like the election season's whimsical changes. The desired transformation of this farcical story, which repeats itself in fiction and nonfiction alike, cannot be achieved except by the transformation of the eternal woman that stares back with stony features and eyes engraved in the eternal memory of the universal pulse. And with it comes the death of the preposterous masculine character that refuses to be humanized and is epitomized in Rustum and in every male aggressor who rapes or otherwise uses women's bodies without remorse. Each and every female character in El Saadawi's novels has undergone a bitter experience of rape or physical abuse in one form or another. The transformation offered in El Saadawi's books is not one to be thought about, but rather one to be experienced. The psychological transformation that her novels provide is one that carves a path into the memory or psyche. It etches change by obliterating the prototypes that have plagued humanity for so long, in life and in fiction, and by ousting their ghosts and laying them to rest for good. To achieve this, El Saadawi concentrates on the importance of the act of writing. By writing things, one makes them real, gives them new life, invigorates them with a new spirit, and liberates them from the heavy biases of past premises and distortions. The act of writing is an act of exorcising the ghosts of the past. In *The Novel* (2009), Carmen summarizes this as she tells the young woman: *Writing is an exercise from birth till death, an exercise spoken without fear, but this is impossible as we live and die in fear, in burning fire and electric shocks and antidepressant pills.* As she hands over her very last novel, her final advice to the young woman is: *There is no deliverance, no hope, except through writing.* This means that the act of writing is an act of dissidence.

CREATIVITY AND DISSIDENCE

The importance of *Diary of a Child Called Souad* lies in the fact that it is an act of dissidence. What El Saadawi wrote years ago as a child was rejected by her school teacher as a punishment for being a dissident. Every word in this diary shows how writing is the one act that exposes the hypocrisy of the socio-political construct we are all endorsing. When the young Souad dies, this is a dissident and creative act in that the young El Saadawi is liberating herself and is saving her novel, first by rejecting a happy ending and killing the traditional role of mother and wife, and second by making the child Souad give life to a baby girl, thus conjoining in her character the fates of all the Eves on earth. In this diary, historical memories are being reshaped, rethought, and recreated as fears and desires that prevent any change are swept away, giving rise to a higher self that has to be born. The plot expands and broadens; it is symbolic of a widening of understanding and motivates change.

A "new order" is a phrase that El Saadawi would disapprove of, because it suggests the New Economic World Order piped by the mass media into the brains of their audience, or the New World Order promised by the senior President Bush. What El Saadawi predicts is a new form that will rise from the ashes of the novel, because the act of writing directly confronts itself in the being of its characters. Writing a novel becomes a supreme act of dissidence. Several characters in El Saadawi's novels struggle with the act of writing in one form or another. They all come in touch with themselves through the act of writing: they either are writers or are becoming writers. This insistence on writing is an insistence on rewriting the history of humanity, the history of slavery and servitude, the history of gender ordeal and abuse, and the history of misrepresentation and misinterpretation of truth. What makes *Diary of a Child Called Souad* appealing is that it is a young girl's unconscious call to change the mentality regarding the liberation of the body and the confidence to act and speak what one desires. The diary exposes the threat of institutionalized education and upbringing that put an end to promising talent such as that found in the young Souad/Nawal. Before Souad is given the chance to explore life, she is married off in her early teens. At the age of 13, she gives birth to a young girl and dies. Since 1944, when little Souad was presented by El Saadawi, we have seen that the social construct she strived to change has remained the same and that the political agenda remains the same as well. In her novels, El Saadawi shows how the global mass movement is present as voices rise in the streets calling for peace, for the liberation of the Palestinian people, and for the sovereignty of the Iraqis. Political crises are manifest in the unheard demands and voices of the masses as preposterous wars go on, forming a major part of the preposterous plot that El Saadawi wants to expose and erase, despite countries calling themselves democratic and claiming to act in the name of the people. El Saadawi sums up all these ideas in her essay *Towards a Philosophy that Will Awaken the Conscience of the Human Race*, saying:

> *We are living in the era of a new colonialism and not in what the ideologists and thinkers of global capitalism describe as post-colonialism, a term which is*

meant to conceal what is really happening. The term "post-colonial" was originally coined by academic circles in the United States and Europe but has been taken over by the intellectual elite in Egypt. It shows how language is used to mystify and mislead people, and reveals how the ruling economic, political and military circles use culture, education and the media to reinforce their power, and control people's minds. (2002: 10)

The question remains: What is so threatening in El Saadawi's writing? Is it the fact that her female protagonists are unfit to represent the liberated spirit of humanity? Do they symbolically threaten religious authorities by being different, rebellious, or a product of some illegitimate relationship, or by often being proud to give birth to an illegitimate child? Is this what the religious authorities are so indignant about? Could young women in fictional novels be so threatening to the fabric of a conservative society by inducing the young generation to emulate their example? The question seems ridiculous, and to answer it would be even more ridiculous. If religious groups and authorities feel threatened on behalf of a moral and virtuous society that might become afflicted and go astray as its plot unfolds, then what of political authorities? It seems to be no coincidence that the banning of one of El Saadawi's novels was concurrent with El Saadawi's candidacy for the Presidency in Egypt against Mubarak. I remember visiting her in her home in Cairo at that time and asking her what would she do if she won the elections. She said: *I am not a politician, I am a writer. Even if I won, if they ever allowed me to win, I would step down. I am only taking this step in order to break apart the divinity of authority, the sacredness of one person staying there with no possibility of a rival, or a change. I want to disrupt that system, to upset it somehow.* Indeed, when demonstrations against the Mubarak regime took place in Egypt, she was among the first to join the people in Tahrir Square and call for change.

It is evident that El Saadawi not only is working for the emancipation of women but also is working for human rights, political rights, for the emancipation of the mind from various veils, and for the emancipation of the act of writing to create a new world. In her *Autobiography Part III*, El Saadawi sums up her hope for a better future to come, as she has devoted the life she has lived and the work she has done for that. She tells her daughter:

I do not believe in a marriage certificate or a certificate in medicine or in literature or a birth or death certificate but I got married with an officially written contract to give my children legitimacy. But today the official marriage certificate is no longer valid. Women are no longer broken and submissive. Most of the educated female youth refuse the official marriage. There are now other forms of unofficial marriage .... Sherif says: "The future will be better than the present Nawal!" I said "But we will not be here Sherif." He said it is not important to be here with our bodies but our ideas will be present in books. I asked in surprise: Do papers have a longer life than human beings? (2001: 213–14)

I think that *Diary of a Child Called Souad* is an answer to this question. The words she wrote with the delicate hands of a child in 1944 are still alive and vibrant in modern times. From that time on, El Saadawi has delivered her word, her message, in the clearest form. *Diary of a Child Called Souad* is about the struggle of all the female characters in her later novels. We see here all of their lives combining, converging into one single being: the young Souad whose little voice creates an outrage in the reader's soul as she has her life stolen away from her in its early rise.

Finally, El Saadawi appears as the teacher inspiring a whole generation. It was Oedipus who was able to bear his fate to expose the reality of his background, and it is El Saadawi who is able to wage a global battle of such a nature to expose the faults and frailties of the whole of humanity. Whereas Oedipus lost the light from his eyes for the revelation of truth, El Saadawi keeps her fire burning and sustains the spirit of generations to come. Her words remain an inspiration and a spur to revolt against any system or individual that hinders the mind and spirit of the people. I last saw El Saadawi in 2012 in Dubai, the United Arab Emirates, as she gave a talk during the Emirates Airline Festival of Literature. After years of struggle she was finally invited to talk in an Arab country, and I remember one thing: as she entered the hall she did not utter a word, but the audience did not stop clapping. At last, she did not need to talk. She had said it all in her books, in her life, and people did not need to hear her words.

They wanted to salute her example. She moved the masses by her sheer presence. Her words had gone so far that now her presence was all that was needed. I looked at her and saw the same luster in her eyes, the same fiery spirit. I felt proud of the receptive crowd. It was certainly a far cry from the crowd I had encountered a decade before in Cairo. With her usual humor she said that she was asked to come on the condition that she edit her words and monitor herself; she smiled and said that she could not. Amid the applause of her audience, I would like to end the answer to my question with a quotation from one of her essays entitled *Democracy, Creativity and African Literature.* Her words here sum up why she no longer needed to talk:

> *Fundamentally, however, the power of creative writing lies in its ability to implant seeds of revolution in the hearts of the oppressed men and women. Revolution is the natural result of creative work, and freedom is the daughter of the revolution. Revolution and freedom, together, constitute the form and content of any creative work. (1997: 207)*
>
> And it is for this very reason that Nawal El Saadawi continues to be banned.

Omnia Amin

REFERENCES

El Saadawi, Nawal. *Memoirs from the Women's Prison.* The Women's Press Limited, 1986.

El Saadawi, Nawal. *Awraqi ... Hayati [My Papers ... My Life]. Part III.* Dar Al Adab, Beirut, Lebanon, 2001.

El Saadawi, Nawal. *The Novel.* Trans. Omnia Amin and Rick London. Interlink Books, Nothampton, Massachusetts, USA, 2009.

El Saadawi, Nawal. *"Towards A Philosophy that Will Awaken the Conscience of the Human Race"* Women and Global Change. 6th International Conference of the Arab Women Solidarity Association (AWSA), 3–5 January 2002, Cairo, Egypt, pp. 9–26.

El Saadawi, Nawal. *"Democracy, Creativity and African Literature"* The Nawal El Saadawi Reader. Zed Books, London and New York, 1997, pp.188–208.

CHAPTER 2

Author's Introduction

While sorting through some old papers in a forgotten drawer in my library, I found one of my notebooks from my first year of secondary school, on which was written: *Composition Homework.*

In 1944, the Arabic language teacher asked us to choose a topic and write three pages about it for the forthcoming composition class. I chose this subject: *Diary of a Child Called Souad.* I spent the entire week writing. I filled the whole notebook and handed it to the teacher. He looked through it, gave me a zero, and returned the notebook to me with instructions to present him with another topic composed of only three pages.

The notebook remained among my papers for almost 45 years until I found it a couple of days ago and read it. I was astonished at how I had written it at that early time of my life, and at how the teacher had given me a zero!

© Omnia Amin 2016, Published by Palgrave Macmillan,   25
A Division of Nature America Inc.
N. El Saadawi, *Diary of a Child Called Souad,*
DOI 10.1007/978-1-137-58730-5

I still remember what he looked like. He was fat and short and wore a creased *tarbush* that fell down to his ears. He held a cane that he used to sting us with. Behind his thick glasses, like the bottoms of bottles, his eyes stood out and gazed at me in anger as he shouted out *Zero!*

Maybe it was this zero that made me stop writing for many years and made me go to medical school instead of the college of literature; maybe if it weren't for my father and mother, my life would have ended like that of Souad.

This is why I decided that I should publish these old papers and present them to every child (female or male) who has thoughts about writing or who develops a desire to do so.

Much early talent is lost because of old, worn-out educational institutions and customs, just as Souad's talent was lost.

Nawal El Saadawi,
Cairo,
March 1990

Diary of a Child Called Souad

CHAPTER 3

Diary of a Child Called Souad

Pleasure floods Souad as she runs over the warm sunny ground. She fills her lungs with pure fresh air and nothing impedes her movement. Her arms, legs, back, neck, and head—everything in her moves; action permeates every cell in her body and mind all at the same time. Her whole being moves, like the parts of one cell in perfect harmony with each other and with the wide universe surrounding it.

She realized a long time ago—she no longer knows when—that this movement induces in her body and mind a strange sort of pleasure. It is more pleasurable than the taste of warm milk that flows in her mouth when her mother touches her, more pleasurable than the warmth of blood that flows in her body when she touches her hand, and more pleasurable than the smooth touch of the ball in her hands.

© Omnia Amin 2016, Published by Palgrave Macmillan,   29
A Division of Nature America Inc.
N. El Saadawi, *Diary of a Child Called Souad*,
DOI 10.1007/978-1-137-58730-5

The minute she catches the ball, she throws it away to run after it and catch it once more. She keeps repeating this and screams with delight. It is the delight of moving arms, legs, back, neck, and head; it is the movement that stirs her body, mind, and the universe around her, with such a peculiar pleasure that makes her laugh out loud as if she were screaming.

Her mother believes she is screaming because she wants the ball, so she picks it up for her and places it in her hands. But Souad becomes angry, cries, and kicks the ball far away. She does not want to hold the ball. Her desire is to move toward it, to move her arms, legs, back, neck, and head. She wants the movement to reach every cell of her body and mind all at the same time, to stir her being as if she were one cell inside this amazing pleasure.

Her mother fails to understand why Souad cries when she places the ball in her hands. She thinks that Souad wants the ball; she does not realize that Souad simply wants to move, and that by giving her the ball she puts an end to her movement. By handing her the ball, she takes away the reason that justifies her action and spoils her pleasure. Her mother would have understood Souad's reason for throwing the ball away the minute she grabbed it if she had only remembered her own childhood, if she had recollected the time when she was the same age as Souad, and if she had recalled that forbidden pleasure she has forgotten—or imagines she has forgotten. It is still stored in some place in her head. When Souad sleeps, she sometimes dreams that she is flying in the air and moves her arms, legs, back, neck, and head with immense pleasure. Her body floats in the universe like a free unhindered bird. She has no clue where she is flying to, but she continues to fly for the sheer pleasure of movement. The spacious universe around her appears to be stretching out, making way for her. She jumps on the tree tops and the roofs of the houses. The night does not frighten her, nor does the sun burn her. She believes that she will continue to swim in the universe forever, but she soon feels her body getting heavier and heavier until it reaches the ground. She attempts to fly once more but cannot. Her body seems stuck to the ground, transfixed. She spots a long shadow heading toward her; his eyes are as red as fire. She tries to move her arms and legs, to run away or fly, but her body does not budge. She attempts to scream but her voice does not come out. The minute the shadow is about to swallow her, she stirs to save her own life and wakes from sleep all sweaty and half-exhausted.

*   *   *

Souad does not yet comprehend that kind of horrific dream or any other dream. She sleeps soundly throughout the night without moving and wakes with a cheerful face. She smiles at her mother's face just as she smiles at the sun and the moon. She does not distinguish between the day and the night, and she is unaware of darkness or fear. She plays with the ball to run and move her arms and legs, or piles the small colored blocks on top of each other. She builds a house bit by bit, and when it reaches the rooftop she shakes it to make sure it is solid, but the walls of the house break down into small blocks. She starts to pile them anew to build the house once more. Her mother sees her as she builds and destroys, builds and destroys, and when she takes the blocks away from her for sleep she cries. She does not want to sleep now. Her mind is still active and occupied with building and destroying, surrendering to this repeated pleasure. She keeps thinking that the walls of the house have become solid and she shakes them, but they fall down. She gives it another go, hoping to build a house that cannot fall down no matter how hard she shook it: a real house like the house she lives in, with real walls like the ones that never fall down when she pushes against them.

She tightly clasps her fingers around one of the blocks. Her mother tries to open her hand and take the block away, but she tightens her grip. When her mother finally succeeds in opening her fingers and taking the block away, she cries. She puts her to bed crying; she sleeps and dreams that her mother is unable to open her hand and the block is still in her grip.

As soon as she opens her eyes in the morning, she looks in her hand and finds nothing. So, she jumps out of bed in search of the box of blocks, but the sound of the bell rings in the street outside the balcony. She runs toward it to find out where it is coming from. The balcony has a high railing that reaches above her head, and the railing has metal bars. She places her head between two bars to look beyond the railing, but her mother pulls her back and screams:

Your head is heavier than your body; you might fall into the street.

But she wants to see where this ringing bell is coming from, and she does not fear falling into the street, and her head is not heavier than her body because she realizes that her body carries her head, her head does not carry her body. The minute her mother disappears inside the kitchen, she runs back to the balcony and places her head between two bars or stands on the tip of her toes so that her head is higher than the railing and she can see the street.

The street seems wide, without beginning or end, and the people walking are as numerous as the stars. The lampposts are tall and have no beginning or end, and cars rush at full speed. The tram has carriages like those of a train and moves on rails and rings with that bell sound that shakes her ears and body with amazing ecstasy. All the sounds in the street sweep her into ecstasy: the car horns with their numerous tunes, the voices of the vendors as they call out, people's steps on the asphalt, the wheels of the tram as they run along the rails, the children's laughter and shouting as they rush along to play.

She places her head between the two bars and wishes to jump in the street and play with them. But her mother pulls her backwards shouting:

You'll fall in the street and die.

But the idea of death has not yet entered her mind. Her mind is still rushing without restrictions, without fear: she wants to move and discover everything. Her body also wants to break from the restrictions of the narrow house and jump from the balcony to move, run, and play in the broad and endless street.

Her father sometimes takes her with him to the street, and she skips with pleasure as she walks beside him. She moves her arms and legs and almost runs, but the big hand grips hers. She tries to pull herself away from her father's grip but is unable to. His long strong fingers surround her like an iron fist that almost suffocates her. She tries to free herself in vain. But the minute the fingers relax a little, she pulls her hand away and runs in the street. Her father runs after her and holds her once more shouting:

Aren't you afraid a car will run you over?

But she remains fearless. She does not fear the street, or the cars, or the people. Her mind jumps without restrictions. It wants to know and discover. Her body moves freely, her arms and legs move as she walks and she feels like she's flying, like a free bird in the air. Her movement is like that of the wind in harmony with the universe, so she and the universe become one. The movement reaches her mind and body all at the same time. It stirs her mind with the pleasure of opening up to life and stirs her body with the pleasure of flying with the movement of the universe.

But her father's hand soon gets hold of her and her small hand falls into the grip of this iron fist that is able to freeze the movement of her body and her mind. She resists for a while and then surrenders. It is not complete surrender because as soon as she feels her father's hand loosening and softening, she rushes away like a small rocket.

When her father buys her a train or a car, she sits on the floor and moves it. She is amazed by the movement and does not know where it comes from, if it is from the bottom of the car or from its front or its back. Her fingers search for the secret and she finds the screws. She undoes them one after the other, and every second she imagines that she will find out the secret; however, the screws are all undone and the car is transformed into small pieces of iron that bear nothing inside. She does the same with the train, and then she searches for her younger sister's toys and her younger brother's. Her sister has only one big doll with a dress made of layers and layers of frills. She takes them off, one after the other, until she reaches the naked body of the doll. She takes off her arms, legs, head, and neck, and she places her fingers in the opening of the neck to find out what is inside, but she only finds air.

Her sister cries when she sees the insides of her torn doll. She pats her and her sister stops crying and they play together. Their younger brother joins them. But her brother is unlike her. He has this small thing between his thighs that her mother calls *the birdie*. She tries to work out the resemblance between it and the bird that flies in the sky, but she finds no resemblance between the two. The bird has wings that flutter in the air, and this one has no wings. She sees that every plane in the sky has wings like the birds, but the train runs on wheels. She pushes the train and it runs on the rails and she laughs with pleasure.

*   *   *

Nothing surmounts the pleasure she gets when she finds herself inside a real train that moves on its own and rushes on the rails with amazing speed. The whistle and steam burst in the atmosphere and the tall lampposts move backwards at a crazy pace. Her eyes are drawn to the movement. She watches its rapidity and seems to pant with the train and its vigorous movement that shakes her body and her mind with amazing pleasure.

The pleasure remains in her mind and body until she reaches her grandmother's house with the big wooden door. She is pleased with the house because it resembles the street. It is as wide as a street and has a sand floor. Her mother sprinkles the floor with water and places the big straw mat on top. She lies on top of it with her Aunt Khadija's children. They roll and tumble and laugh. She leaves the straw mat and rolls on the ground. Her face and hair get filled with dust. She fills her palms with it and places it in her mouth. She chews and swallows it with pleasure.

But her mother pulls her from behind and with a sharp voice screams in her ears:

Don't eat the mud or your stomach will hurt you.

She cries and kicks and her grandmother comes and pats her on her back with her familiar dark hand. She brings her face next to hers to kiss her and she smells pastries, milk, and dust. She sees her toothless mouth and her eyes that have no eyelashes, her dark wrinkled complexion, and her bald head, which she covers with one black scarf on top of another. Unlike her mother, she has no breasts. Her wide black dress falls down to the ground. Souad pulls the scarf away from her granny's head to see if she has any hair. Red hair with grey roots appears, but her granny pulls the scarf back on top of her head and covers it. Souad asks her:

Where have your teeth gone, Granny, and your breasts?

Her grandmother laughs until her eyes water and she wipes them with the tip of her scarf and says:

The ghoul has eaten them, my love.

Her Aunt Khadija's children gather around her, saying:

Tell us the story of the ghoul, Granny.

Up to this point Souad has not been afraid of her grandmother, but now she becomes afraid of her wide and toothless mouth when she tells them about the ghoul, with her wrinkled dark face becoming darker and darker in the night. In the middle of the night when she suddenly wakes up to pee, she shivers and remains lying in her place. She imagines that the ghoul will pounce on her body under the cover. She pulls the cover over her face so that the ghoul would not see her, and she closes her eyes and sleeps. The pee presses against the wall of her bladder as she sleeps, and she dreams that she has run to the toilet. In the morning she finds her clothes wet and the straw mat underneath her wet, so she creeps from under the cover on the tips of her toes to the wide court-yard of the house inundated by the sun. She stands in the sun to get dry but the minute she hears the donkey bray and the voice of her aunt's husband as he leads the donkey from the stable, she runs to him and hangs on the donkey to ride it and go to the field.

In the field she runs among the maize and orange trees. She pulls the hoe from her cousin Zaki and hits the ground as her Uncle Abdullah does. She runs after Zaki and grabs him by his *galabiya* that resembles a girls' *galabiya*. Zaki gathers some of the dry ears of corn and lights a fire to barbeque the corn and eat; but they soon hear the noise of the waterwheel, so they run to it and ride on the wheel, going round and round with it and screaming.

Her screams show her pleasure, that feeling she knows well when she moves her bare feet on the warm ground satiated with the sun and the pure air fills her chest. Nothing impedes her body's move-ment. Her motion is part of the movement of the universe, as if she were swimming or flying in this limitless space.

She returns home on the donkey's back. The smell of baking and pastries comes from the house. She runs to sit on the low table beside her cousins. She eats with them from the same plate. But her mother pulls her by the hand and takes her to the courtyard where the big earthenware pot of water stands. She pours out water from a jug for her to wash her hands. She then sits beside her sister and brother at another low table laid out especially for them, where they all eat from their own plates.

She watches her cousins eat from far away and she exchanges glances with Zaki. They smile across the distance that divides them. She asks her mother why she is not allowed to eat with her cousins. Her mother whispers in her ear that they are peasants and they eat with their dirty hands from one plate.

But she wants to eat with Zaki more than she wants to eat with her brother and sister. She loves playing with Zaki more than with them. Zaki knows many things and rides the donkey on his own. He knows the way to the field on his own and has many friends among the neighbors, who play together in the street or walk on the Nile Bridge until the sun sets and it becomes dark, whereupon they sit in front of the house by the light of the moon. They narrate stories she has never heard before. Stories about the ghost that appears at night in the form of a tall giant with red eyes, or in the form of a humongous black cat that meows, or a wolf that howls in a strange way, or in the form of a big fish with the head of a woman whom they call the Jinni as she comes out from the middle of the Nile and walks on the bridge at night. If she finds people, she kidnaps them and takes them to the bottom of the Nile. Souad pants as she listens to these stories and the darkness around her fills with ghosts, so she moves close to where Zaki sits on the ground and clings to him as she rolls herself into a ball, hiding her arms and legs under her body, fearing that the ghost will pull her far away.

Her Aunt Khadija comes, and when she finds her sitting on the ground with the boys she tells her:

> *If your mother sees you sitting on the ground like this she will beat you.*

She envies Zaki because his mother does not beat him if he sits on the floor, and she tells her:

> *Why don't you beat Zaki: he is sitting on the floor like me?*

Her Aunt Khadija laughs and covers her mouth with the tip of her black scarf and says:

> *Zaki is a peasant, the son of your Uncle Abdullah, who is a peasant, and your aunt is a peasant; but you are a city girl and your mother is a city woman and your father is a big government employee.*

She does not know yet what the words *peasant* and *city* imply, not even the word *employee*. But she thinks that her Aunt Khadija loves her more than she loves her son Zaki or any of her other children. But she loves her brother more than her because she gives him the donkey to ride and does not give it to her. She tells her:

The boy rides and the girl walks, because girls have iron in their feet.

She looks at her own feet and legs and searches for the iron. Her aunt laughs and covers her mouth with her scarf and says:

I mean, my dear, that a girl endures more than a boy.

So she asks her:

Does this mean that a girl is stronger than a boy, Auntie?

Her aunt answers:

A girl has seven lives like the cats, but a boy has only one life.

She does not understand what her aunt means, but she says:

This means that a girl is better than a boy.

Her aunt answers immediately:

No, my love, a boy is better than ten girls.

Souad notices that Zaki is wearing a girl's *galabiya*, so she tells her aunt:

If a boy is better than a girl, then why is Zaki wearing a girl's galabiya? And why does a girl have seven lives and a boy has one?

Her aunt answers:

Because a boy is easily harmed. People quickly envy him and he becomes ill and dies when he is little. I lost three boys before Zaki. Your grandmother told me: "Khadija, people in this small village have eyes like bullets aimed at the boy. As for a girl, no one envies her." A girl brings burdens but a boy brings happiness to his family. And a boy who wears a girl's galabiya is not envied, as people think he is a girl. I have three boys and five burdensome girls. They are a heavy burden on the heart.

Souad is amazed as her aunt speaks poorly of girls and she tells her:

But Auntie, you are a girl, so do you hate yourself, too?

Her aunt laughs and says:

My love, I swear you have a clever brain. God has created me a woman and I am content with my fate. What can I do? This is God's will. It is God who creates a girl and He is the one who creates a boy.

Souad feels that God loves her brother more than her, because He created him a boy and not a girl. Her brother starts to like playing with boys like himself and they send the girls out of the game. She cries when he sends her out as well and she goes home and complains. Her father tells her:

Don't play in the street with the boys.

Souad does not like going back to the small apartment that is filled with furniture and has no spacious courtyard. There is no field to run in, no donkey to ride, and no street to play in with the boys and sit on the ground by the light of the moon telling stories about those strange and magical worlds.

The street below the balcony is filled with cars, people, vendors, and the tram. She doesn't go down to the street to play. Her mother always warns her against going out of the apartment door on her own, because in the street there are strange men who steal children away.

Souad wanders in the three small rooms of the house like a little prisoner. She takes her toys out of the box to play with her sister and brother, or with any children who might come with their parents to visit her mother and father.

The sound of the tram's bell keeps drawing Souad's attention toward the balcony. She stands on the doorstep leading to the balcony and looks at the neighboring balcony, where a woman sits combing her long, black hair. When she sees her she smiles, and she notices her large, wide mouth like that of the ghoul. So she runs inside the house and screams:

The ghoul!

Her mother tells her that she is not the ghoul but their neighbor, but she is unable to go out to the balcony on her own. She thinks that the minute she goes near the balcony this woman will reach out between the metal railings with her hand or her long hair and grab her and eat her.

She is reminded of her old pleasure of going out with her father in the street. She walks beside him and moves her arms and legs and feels the urge to jump and fly. But she resists the temptation, for the street is filled with cars, and one of the cars might run her over. She holds her father's hand and clings to him. She is afraid to let go of him in the midst of the crowds and lose him among the people. She does not know the way home, and she would get lost in the wide streets that stretch out endlessly. The night would fall and she would be walking on her own in the dark and she would not find her room and her bed where she hides under the cover from the ghosts. She would not find her mother who places her arm around her until she sleeps. She would cry from fear and hunger, and one of the thieves who steals children would see her and take her and no one would know where she is.

She twists her small fingers around her father's hand. If she accidentally slips away from him in the crowds, she runs and holds his hand before she loses it. But when she is near the house and sees her mother looking at them from the balcony, she leaves her father's hand and runs on her own. She climbs the stairs by herself and knocks hard on the door.

Riding the train also reminds her of her old pleasure and this fast movement that puts her body in ecstasy. Her mind wonders why the lampposts run behind while the train runs to the front, and why

the lampposts run on the ground without wheels
and without any rails like the train. But her father
tells her that the lamps are fixed in the ground and
do not move. She is amazed as she sees them run
behind but the minute the train stops, they too
stop.

This time she sees neither her grandmother's
house with the big wooden door, nor her Aunt
Khadija and her children, nor the field, nor the
donkey. She sees a big house surrounded by a garden and a big metal door with a bell at the top. It
rings whenever the door opens or closes.

She goes in after her mother and sister.
Behind her are her father and brother. A big dog
approaches barking and exposing long pointed
fangs. She clings to her mother in fear. But her
mother shouts at the dog and tells him off:

Go away, wolf.

The dog immediately calms down and rubs its
nose against her mother's plump pale leg so she
pats him on the head. The dog goes round them
one by one, smelling them from the front and from
behind. She freezes in her place when the dog licks
her foot. She fears that if she moves her leg he will
open his mouth and eat it. In her Uncle Abdullah's
field there was a dog; but it was not as huge as this
one, and its mouth was not as big or as scary as this
mouth. Its barking wasn't frightening or rough like
this one's either.

A short, slim man approaches. He has grey hair
and his voice is loud and rough. He wears yellow

silk pajamas with a green silk robe over them. She hears her mother tell her:

Say hello to your grandfather, Souad.

Her grandfather kisses her on the cheek. She smells something strange. It is unlike her father's smell or her mother's or her grandmother's. It is a mixture of smoke, cologne, and something else like the spirit-cooker. A tall, young man with a pale face and thick black hair arrives. Her mother says:

Say hello to your Uncle Hasanein.

She shakes hands and hears his loud, rough voice that resembles her grandfather's.

She finds her grandfather's house spacious, with many rooms and a lot of furniture. The floor is sparkling and has thick carpets on it. The walls are colored, with many pictures hanging on them in thick golden frames. She hears her father call her grandfather *Ali Bey* and her grandfather call her father *Hassan Effendi*.

As for her grandmother, she is silent all the time. She sits with her full, pale body wrapped in a black silk dress. Her thick, pale legs are covered by transparent black stockings. She has a round, pale face and her complexion is sagging, but she has no wrinkles. Her eyes are unlike other people's eyes. She does not have any black or white in them but all one color: grey. They look as if they have never seen the light or the sun, or as if their black has melted into their white from lots of crying or lots of sleep. Her plump, pale hands rest in her lap. They are small but sagging from waiting for a time longer than time itself.

She never sees her grandmother except sitting quietly in a corner of the spacious hall. She looks with her grey eyes from time to time at the patch of light that appears when the door of the house opens. As for her Aunt Dawlat, she sees her move in the house only from one room to the other, speaking in a loud voice to the maid. Her aunt does not have a pale complexion like her mother. She isn't plump, but slim and dark and short like her grandfather. Her voice is loud like his and she has wide eyes with a lot of white and a small black bit moves quickly inside the white. It is like the movement of her lips when she speaks or the movement of her hands and arms as she walks behind the maid from one room to the next, rebuking her for not cleaning the windows as she should, or for not setting the sheets on the bed as she trained her to, or for not removing the dust from the big radio that is the size of a cupboard that stands in a corner of the hall.

That radio is the only thing that Souad likes in her grandfather's house. She has never seen a radio before. When her uncle turns one of its knobs, singing and music shoot out of it. Her eyes widen in astonishment and curiosity. Beside the radio there is another big cupboard that they call the *phonograph*. It has a wooden handle on one side that her uncle turns and the record goes round, and on top of the record a thin needle goes round, and singing and music come out.

The minute the garden doorbell rings, her uncle removes the needle from the top of the record and silence fills the wide hall. Her uncle's loud voice ceases and the maid hides in the kitchen. Everything inside the spacious house becomes quiet and does not stir from its place. Even her grandmother becomes more silent and her grey eyes stop moving as her gaze becomes fixed. She comes to resemble a statue made of wax with her black dress and pale body.

Later, she realizes that the sound of the bell means that her grandfather has opened the door and come in. Her grandfather has a specific movement when he opens the door, which makes the bell ring with a certain tone that all the family members know. His shoes have a specific rhythm on the stairs at the house entrance. His small cane has a knob that resembles a snake's head. He uses it to knock on the glass of the outside door, then he enters the hall with his slim, short body and his large, pale head. His loud breathing as he moves announces his arrival, as well as that cough or clearing of the throat or blowing his nose or his loud voice when he calls out for his son, his daughter, or the maid to take the cane from him and carry his coat or help him take off his jacket and hang it on a hanger.

He never calls out for his wife. Souad imagines that her grandfather and grandmother do not talk at all with each other. And that her uncle does not speak to her aunt, and that the only talking that takes place inside the house is between her aunt and the maid or the cook in the kitchen. This is not talk, but rather orders or angry comments.

Souad does not like the days at her grandfather's house. The garden is spacious and has beautiful flowers, but Wolf, the dog, awaits her every time she gets ready to go down there, unless the gardener ties him up with a chain. When she goes down there, her shoes get dirtied with mud and her Aunt Dawlat's eyes watch her footsteps when she climbs back from the garden into the hall, and her loud and angry voice rings in the house announcing that the floor of the hall is dirty.

She has nothing else to do but sit beside the radio when her uncle moves the needle and the singing and music start. She follows her uncle's fingers, attempting to discover the secret. How can the sound come out of this wooden cupboard? One time she got so curious and reached out and moved the needle in her uncle's absence. Her body stirs with a peculiar ecstasy when a man's voice starts to sing. She almost screams with pleasure, but her uncle's voice falls on her ears like thunder:

Don't touch the radio or you'll break it!

She shrivels in her big seat in the hall. Her aunt with her protruding angry eyes approaches, her shoes tapping on the floor of the hall. She extends her large, dark hand and with her thin, shaking fingers she switches off the radio.

At night before she goes to sleep, she whispers in her mother's ear:

When will we go back to our house, Mama?

Her mother pats her and says:

When your father's holiday is over.

She puts her arms around her and says:

But I don't like it here.

Her mother says:

Why, Souad? The garden here is beautiful and your grandfather's house is spacious, not like our cramped house.

Souad says:

But I don't like my grandfather.

Her mother places her hand over her mouth and whispers to her:

Don't say this in front of anyone here. Your grandfather loves you and you have to love him, Souad.

She closes her eyes and sleeps. She wakes up in the middle of the night. She doesn't find her mother beside her in bed, nor her sister, nor her brother. She is completely alone and thick darkness surrounds her. Her eyes search in the dark for a spot of light. She sees shadows move on the wall. Black shadows with red eyes like the ghosts. She hides her head under the cover and wraps her arms and legs around her stomach. But the pee presses on her bladder and hurts her. She raises the cover a little and peeps out to get up and walk to the bathroom. But the strange shadows are still waiting for her by the door. Behind the door there is a long, dark corridor and the bathroom is far away. It has an open window that overlooks the garden and, who knows, maybe a shadow or ghost will jump through the window, or a thief, and take her away where no one will know where she is. She hides her head once more under the cover and closes her eyes and goes to sleep. She sees herself play in the garden and the pee is pressing on her bladder as she plays so she runs to the back stairs that lead to the bathroom and sits down and pees. She feels the pleasure of the warm pee and the pain that presses against her stomach completely disappears with the last warm drop. She suddenly opens her eyes and quickly places her hand underneath her. When she feels the wetness she jerks with fear. She tries to sleep once more, but the wetness underneath her makes her feel cold. She places a bit of the cover between her and the wetness but she does not sleep. A question lingers and spreads fear in her heart: what will her aunt do when she sees her bed in the morning?

She does not want the morning to come and prays to God that the night will last until her bed dries. She rolls the bedspread underneath her so it will soak up the wetness; but the morning comes and nothing is dry. She does not leave her bed and stays hidden under the cover until her aunt arrives with the maid behind her to clean the room. She slips from her bed, escaping to her mother's and father's room. But she soon hears her aunt's loud voice echoing in all the rooms of the house, announcing that she's wet the bed. She hides in the wardrobe in her mother's room.

But her aunt manages to find her and she drags her out of the wardrobe saying:

Come out, you peasant, you bed wetter!

She does not know what the word *peasant* means, but it gets connected in her mind with a feeling of shame because she wet the bed. She starts to cry whenever her aunt tells her:

You're a peasant.

She feels ashamed even if she does not wet the bed.

* * *

Souad finds herself in another house without a balcony and without a wide street to see from the balcony. Instead, it has a big window overlooking another high building, and at the window there are metal railings. Her head has grown and cannot pass between the railings, so she starts to press her face between two of the railings to look at the narrow street under her window. A man stands beside a cart with piles of peanuts and pumpkin seeds. In the middle of the cart there is a black chimney emitting thick smoke. Its color fades as it rises and disappears in the atmosphere.

Her eyes are fixed on the last trails of smoke in the air. She sees the blue sky radiant with the light of the sun, and a bird fluttering in the golden light, flying with this peculiar free movement that she does not possess. If God had created her a bird, wouldn't this have been far better? She would have been able to slip with her small body between these railings and fly in the air without her mother or father seeing her and without having to open the locked apartment door.

Her mother always keeps the door locked. She hears her say that there are many thieves. At night she firmly locks the windows. She doesn't know how a thief could slip between the metal railings at the windows while she could not slip out between them. But she does not distinguish much between a thief and a ghost. A ghost, as she hears from her aunt, has no body, but is a spirit that no one can see. The ghost might change its looks and become long and thin like a snake and enter through any crack in the door or the window. It could also be huge, with a big head that is bigger than an elephant's, with red eyes like burning embers.

She does not like the night because the night is dark and ghosts only appear in the dark. She likes the daytime and the sun when it shines and fills the world with light and warmth. But the high building next to them blocks the sun and she cannot see it except far away in the sky. Its golden rays fall near her window but do not come inside. She reaches out her arms between the railings but her hand cannot reach it.

The thing she likes most is to go out of the house into the street with her father or mother. The street is the same street she saw before. It is wide and endless, without a beginning or an end. The cars rush over the shiny asphalt road and many people walk there. The vendors call out, car horns toot, and bicycle bells ring. She realizes that this street is not the old street, because the old street had a tram that ran on rails and this street has no tram.

One day, Souad finds herself at school. She cries on the first day when her mother leaves her on her own among strange faces. She fears that someone might steal her, but the day comes to an end and no one steals her away. Her father arrives and takes her home. She remains scared the following day because of the unfamiliar faces, and she imagines that some-one will take her to a faraway place and her father will not know where she is; but the day comes to an end, and her father arrives and takes her home.

Souad becomes familiar with the faces at school. She comes to know the faces of the other children in her class and she knows the face of the teacher who teaches them the letters of the alphabet. In class, a child called Mohamed sits beside her. He carries a plastic bag with a piece of cake in his schoolbag. He gives her a piece of it. She feels hungry so she eats it. She starts to play with Mohamed in the school yard. They slide together and ride the swing.

One day, she goes up to class from the school yard before everyone else. She feels hungry. She sees Mohamed's schoolbag beside her own so she opens it, takes out the piece of cake, and places it in her mouth before anyone sees her. Mohamed comes and opens his schoolbag. He cannot find the piece of cake and looks around and wonders:

Who took my cake?

The teacher hears him as she passes between the rows so she says in a loud voice that fills the classroom:

Who took Mohamed's cake?

Her voice is as loud as her aunt's, and the thin cane waves between her thin, shaky, and pointed fingers. Souad firmly seals her lips and holds her breath so that the smell of the cake might not come out from her mouth. Her heart beats fast and her fingers shiver on the paper as she holds the pen.

But the class is over and the teacher leaves the classroom without finding out who took the cake. The day comes to an end and she returns home. She knows the way from the house to the school and can go to school alone. She walks fast as if she is running. She wants to reach home in the shortest time possible before anyone kidnaps her. Her fear intensifies when she sees the old beggar who looks at her with narrow searching eyes and then walks behind her with his wooden cane. Souad runs with utmost speed. Every morning her mother places in her schoolbag a plastic bag with half a loaf filled with either a boiled egg or a piece of cheese. She eats it when she gets hungry, but it never satisfies her. Sometimes when she is in class alone, she opens Mohamed's schoolbag and quickly gobbles the piece of cake before anyone sees her.

Mohamed lives in a tall building next door. He sometimes calls to her from his high window to play in the street in front of the house. Her mother opens the door of the apartment and says:

Don't play far away from the house so you won't get lost or anyone steals you away.

At the end of the day, her mother goes out with her father and locks the apartment. She hits the door with all her might and screams, wanting to open it. The door remains closed and her hand hurts. At times one of her fingers might get hurt or her palm might swell and become red. She leaves the door and goes inside to play with her sister and brother or with Fathiya the maid.

Fathiya is a little older than her. Her head has no hair after her mother shaved it all off because it was full of lice. She wears a headscarf like the ones her grandmother and aunt wear, but it is not black. Souad never plays with Fathiya, except when her mother goes out. She pulls her by her wide *galabiya* as she stands by the sink washing dishes, saying:

Come, let's play, Fathiya.

But Fathiya remains in her place and says:

No Miss Souad, Madam will beat me.

So she tells her:

Mama has gone out with Baba.

Fathiya dries her wet hands on her *galabiya* and then goes out with her to the hall or to her room where they play hide and seek, or she squats on the floor and arranges her legs under her *galabiya* and tells her stories about the ghosts she heard from her grandmother and cousins. Once she asked Fathiya where the ghosts come from, and she told her that ghosts appear after a person dies and her father's ghost came out after he died. Her mother saw him standing by the door of the stable so she screamed in fear.

She did not know that Fathiya, just like her and like other people, had a father and a mother. She thought she had come from the street, so she asks her:

Do you have a mother, Fathiya, and she gave birth to you just like my mother gave birth to me?

Fathiya says:

Of course, Miss Souad, everyone in the world has a mother who gave birth to them.

Souad asks:

And everyone has a father?

Fathiya says:

Of course, everyone in the world has a father, because the mother cannot become pregnant and have a child without a father.

Her lips part in amazement because she imagined that she knew this already, but another question gathers in her mind:

How does the mother become pregnant and the child go inside her stomach?

Fathiya laughs and hides her mouth with her hand with the same movement her aunt makes to hide her mouth with the tip of her scarf when she laughs. She says:

The father sleeps with the mother and the mother's belly becomes bigger as the child grows inside. After 9 months the child is born. All of us are born after 9 months, Miss Souad.

The key turns in the lock of the front door and Fathiya jumps in fear and says:

Madam has returned!

And she runs to the kitchen. Her mother and father come in and her mother takes her to bed to sleep and asks her why she is awake at this late hour. But she does not tell her that she played with Fathiya, and she closes her eyes and feigns sleep. Her mother thinks she is asleep, so she goes out of the room on tiptoe.

It is a Friday morning, and every Friday she rides in the horse carriage and goes to the sea with everyone in the house, including Fathiya. Fathiya carries the big basket filled with food and walks behind them. Her feet sink into the sand and is usually way behind them. Her mother turns around from time to time and tells her to catch up.

Souad does not know how to swim yet, but she plays in the sand with her sister and brother. Sometimes she flings herself in the water to swim like the other children, but her mother pulls her back and her loud voice rings in her ears:

You will drown and die!

She does not yet know the meaning of death. The minute her mother turns around, she throws herself in the water and moves her arms and legs with all her might. She wishes that she could swim in the water the way a bird flies in the air. But her body soon becomes heavy and the water goes into her nose and mouth. She puts her hands on the floor and stands on her feet, then thrusts herself forward once more and tries to move her arms and legs.

She almost succeeds in swimming, but her mother pulls her from behind as she screams:

You will drown and die!

She sits beside her under the umbrella and plays in the sand with her sister and brother. When she feels hungry, her mother calls for Fathiya, who takes some food out for her from the basket.

Fathiya sits close to them with the food basket beside her. When her mother and father go to swim in the sea, she runs and sits beside her to tell her stories. One time she catches her crying and asks her the reason. Fathiya tells her that she wants to see her mother and thinks that if she walks on the beach to its very end she will find the way to her village. But she is afraid that the beach might be too long, or that she would not find her village in the end and night would fall and she would have to sleep alone in the dark and a kidnapper might steal her or one of the ghosts might come upon her. But she thinks that if she starts to walk in the early morning, she will reach her village before the sun sets.

The following day, Souad opens her eyes and she hears her mother's loud voice saying:

Fathiya has run away.

Her father puts on his suit and tarbush and goes out to inform the police. The day ends and night falls and Fathiya does not return. Souad closes her eyes to sleep and sees Fathiya walk along the long beach until the end. The night falls before Fathiya reaches her mother, and she sleeps on the beach on her own in the silence of the night. Then, a thief comes to her and steals her or a jinni comes out of the sea and attacks her. Souad's mother hears her get up scared from her sleep in the middle of the night screaming:

Fathiya!

She goes to her bed and lies down beside her and pats her on her back and asks her about what

frightened her. She tells her that Fathiya said she
would walk along the beach until the end, and
there she would find her village and see her mother.

Her mother quickly jumps up from her side
saying:

Did she tell you this?

She says in a scared voice:

Yes.

Her mother shouts:

*And why didn't you tell us this as we were searching
for her all day?*

She closes her lips in fear. She sees her mother
hurry to her father. Her father takes off his night
shirt and puts on his suit and tarbush and goes out.

In the morning, Fathiya comes in with a police-
man holding her hand. Her body is trembling and
her eyes are wet with tears. Her father takes the
thin whip and says to her:

Why did you escape?

Fathiya opens her mouth to answer but her voice
does not come out and her father keeps hitting her
until she stops screaming.

Souad hides in her room under the bed. She
is afraid of her father. She did not think Fathiya
would survive because of the thieves, or that she

would return to them. She does not know how the thieves let her go. She imagines that they left her because she is a poor servant who has no mother—for thieves only steal what is valuable. She imagines that her mother fears for her because she is valuable and she feels some sort of inner pride that soon disappears as she remembers that the more precious she becomes, the more she is in danger of being stolen by thieves. She envies Fathiya, but this envy soon disappears as she hears her scream because she is being beaten. She is grateful to God because He did not create her a servant like Fathiya, who is being beaten by her father and mother and made to wash the floor and the dishes and sleep on the floor in the kitchen and eat the leftovers. Fathiya also has to live away from her mother and is unable to see her mother every day like she does. She hears her father's angry voice call out to her, so she comes out from under the bed, trembling. She goes to her father who is standing tall and wide in the hall, eyes red with anger and with long, shaking fingers twisted round the whip. She hears him say:

Why didn't you tell us what Fathiya told you?

He stings her with the whip on her arms and legs as he says:

Don't hide anything from us ever again.

She answers in a shaking voice:

Yes.

And runs to her mother for protection.

She jumps with joy when she hears the voice of her friends Samira or Mohamed call out to her. She runs to play with them in the street and to buy a bag of pumpkin seeds from the man who stands with a cart. She loves pumpkin seeds, but her mother refuses to give her any money and tells her:

Don't eat from the street as your stomach will hurt you.

Every time, she fills her hands with pumpkin seeds and eats them and feels no stomach pain. On the contrary, she enjoys the salty, tasty flavor. When playing hide and seek with Mohamed and Samira in front of the house, she hides under the porter's bench so that Mohamed and Samira will not see her. The porter is a tall man with a dark face and wears a big white head turban. When he sees her father come in or go out, he rises from his bench and raises his hand to his head in greeting as he says:

Good morning, Bey.

Souad realizes that her father is a respectable man because the porter calls him *Bey,* just like her father calls her grandfather *Ali Bey.*

Souad, Mohamed, and Samira sit on the wooden bench near the door and the porter tells them about his faraway village near Aswan at the end of the Nile. He tells them that he used to swim in the Nile when he was a child and catch fish and grill it on the fire. Her mother sees her sit beside the porter so she pulls her by the arm and takes her inside the house and tells her:

> *Don't sit again with the porter. He is sick in the chest and his germs might get passed on to you through his cough and his breath.*

Souad does not know what germs are, but she imagines small things as thin as snakes. So every time she comes close to the bench where the porter sits, she runs holding her breath with her hand over her nose and mouth.

Every time she comes back from school, she walks quickly as if she is running. She just wants to reach home before one of the child-stealers kidnaps her. The distance between the school and the house seems quite long. The street is wide and appears without beginning or end, and the people's faces seem strange. She tries not to look at them, but looks in front of her as her mother tells her to. If someone smiles at her or tries to talk to her, she does not answer because those thieves have many ways of attracting children to them.

One day while walking fast with her eyes fixed in front of her, neither diverting to the left nor to the right or back, she hears a strange voice from behind her. It sounded as scary as thunder. She turns back instinctively and sees the street filled with a massive number of men. They were violently stamping the ground with their shoes and their eyes were staring with anger, waving fists in the air, and shouting together in one voice some incomprehensible words.

Her body shakes with fear and she thinks they are going to pounce on her, so she runs in panic until she finds an open door of some house and hides behind it. She hears a woman's voice tell her:

Don't be afraid my child. They will not do anything to you.

Her words do not pacify her. On the contrary, her unfamiliar voice adds to her panic and she thinks she is going to kidnap her. But her body remains transfixed behind the door, unable to move and wet with sweat. She continues to hide behind the door until the men's voices dwindle away. She then comes out of her hiding place and shoots out like a rocket until she reaches home full of dread. Her mother asks her about what happened and she tells her what she saw. Her mother laughs and says:

It is a demonstration against the English.

This is the first time she has heard the word *English*. She asks her father who the English are and he tells her that the English are our enemies. She asks him:

Are the English people like us?

Her father says that they are people like us but their faces are white and red with blood and they are infidels and not Muslims like us. They steal our country's money and shoot us with bullets when we tell them to get out of our country and to go back to theirs.

Most things around her induce dread, and the world outside the house is filled with fears and dangers. The thing that scares her most is to get lost in the street and not find her father or mother. Her father no longer holds her hand as he walks beside her, and her eyes remain fixed on him in fear that he will disappear in the street crowd. Her father's legs are long and his step is broad. She is unable to catch up with him unless she runs. Her father's step is faster than hers. Her eyes remain fixed on her father's back, but she fears she might lose him amid the masses. The street is wide and full of people, and the men's backs resemble her father's. Her father gets lost from her in the crowd and her eyes stare with panic as if she were drowning in a big sea where no one knows her and no one can save her. She imagines many strange eyes surrounding her, so she runs and screams out:

Baba!

Her father hears her scream from behind so he looks back quickly, and the minute her eyes fall on his face she rushes to him and holds his hand and does not let go of it another time.

On the beach, her mother no longer holds her hand. She leaves her to swim in the water in front of her. But she does not go too far away from her; if she does goes far, her eyes remain fixed on her mother's face as she sits under the umbrella. She fears she will lose her among other faces and fail to find where she is. If she goes in the water, she remains next to the shore. She moves her arms and legs in the water and then quickly stands on her feet to make sure that the ground is still beneath her. Each time she fears she might stand up and not find the ground underneath her and drown in the sea.

In bed, she never goes to sleep unless she holds her mother's hand and twists her fingers around hers. Every time, sleep overcomes her and her fingers loosen from around her mother's, and her mother gets up quietly; but she hears the sound of the bed shifting and realizes that her mother is leaving her, so she grips her hand once more and does not let go of her. Her mother sings to her in a soft voice or tells her the story of Little Red Riding Hood until she is completely overcome by sleep, and when she slips her hand away her fingers remain loose and lose their grip. So her mother rises, covers her, switches off the lights, and goes to her room.

She does not feel her leave, but she dreams that she lost her mother in the street and she cannot find her, and that she remains lost in the street crying until she sees her father's face and jumps from joy and holds his hand. But her father's hand slips away and he, too, gets lost in the crowd. Strange, wide eyes surround her on all sides, and strange, wide mouths. She becomes afraid and retreats to hide in the house. But she does not find her mother in the house. She finds another strange woman with long hair and a mouth as wide as the ghoul's. She tells her that her mother is dead. She tries to scream but her voice does not come out. In extreme panic, she wakes up abruptly. She finds herself alone in the dark, so she calls her mother in a loud voice: *Mama* ... When she sees her mother's face, she realizes that she was dreaming and becomes happy because her mother did not die. In the morning, she forgets the dream completely as if it never took place.

* * *

At school she likes the recess and does not like class. During recess she runs and plays and moves her arms and legs, but in class she sits still with a paper and pen in front of her. The teacher passes along the rows and her long, thin fingers twist around a cane with which she stings any child who speaks without permission or moves away from his seat or laughs. She tells them that laughter without a reason is ill manners. Every time she thinks of something funny she closes her lips or hides her head in her notebook. She thinks of funny things and sometimes she laughs for no reason, just because Mohamed or Samira looks at her, or when her pen falls on the floor and makes a loud sound, or if one of the pupils sneezes loudly, or if her neighbor's stomach produces sounds like a cat's meows, or the intestines of one of them produces wind with that muffled whistle.

The thing she hates the most in class is to sit still in her place without moving. She sometimes raises her hand and tells the teacher that she wants to go to the toilet so she will give her permission to go out. She quickly rises from her seat and runs in the courtyard and feels great pleasure in moving her arms and legs, opening her mouth and filling it with air and laughter. She wonders to herself if there should be a reason for movement and a reason for laughter. And why they prevent her from laughter and from movement that fills her body with pleasure. Isn't pleasure enough reason for laughter and movement?

But she starts to realize that the old pleasure she used to feel when she ran or laughed is no longer the same. A slow and mysterious feeling starts to fill her because sheer pleasure is forbidden or taboo, and there needs be another reason other than pleasure to justify movement, laughter, or play. She is 7 years old and the month of Ramadan starts. Her father tells her that he started fasting and praying when he was her age. Fasting seems to her a new and exquisite game. The best thing about it is that the imposed system and times for sleep and waking are turned upside down. So that the night, which is for sleep, becomes for waking and eating, and the streets and houses remain awake and the lights are switched on and songs rise from the radio. The *Mesaharaty* comes and beats his drum to wake people and her mother prepares food. She sees various types of tasty food she has not seen before, and new types of sweets: *konafa, katayef,* apricot sheets, nuts, almonds, walnuts, and trays of rice and fried meat. As she eats her food, she wonders why the month of Ramadan is called the fasting month, and her father tells her because people abstain from eating the whole month.

Why do people fast, Father?
Because God has ordered them to fast, my daughter.
And why has God ordered them to fast, Father?
Because God wants them to feel hungry and know how the poor suffer.

Souad fills her stomach with food and tells her father:

But Father, I don't feel hungry and I feel that I eat and satisfy my hunger more than any other time.

Her father's mouth at this point is filled with food and is holding a fried piece of meat that he is about to raise to his mouth. It shakes a bit in his hand before he puts it in his mouth. He can't open his mouth to answer his daughter's question and he waits until he has chewed his food and swallowed it and then says:

But my daughter, we eat only at night and fast all day for the whole month of Ramadan. In the other months we eat during the day.

Souad said:

And we fast at night, Father, because we sleep at night and we do not eat like we're eating now.

Her father remains quiet for a while then says to her:

This is true, Souad, but we do not feel hungry at night because we cannot feel during sleep; but in the morning we feel hungry and thirsty, especially during the hot days.

She imagines that the poor can be hungry but they can never be thirsty because water is in abundance and flows for free from taps, in the sea, in the Nile, and in the canals. She asks in astonishment:

Do the poor also get thirsty, Father?

Her father has finished his food, so he gets up and only her mother is left finishing her food with a piece of *konafa* filled with raisins and almonds. She asks her:

Do the poor get thirsty, Mother?

Her mother says with her mouth full:

They only become hungry, but God wants us to become hungry and thirsty during Ramadan in order to feel the pain of thirst and hunger and as a result have pity on the poor. He wants us to love them and share some of what He has given us with them. He also wants us to be grateful for the food we have. Is it God who gave us food, Mother? Yes, my daughter, God gives and denies to whomever He wants.

Why did God give to us, Mother?
Because God loves us, Souad.

Souad feels some sort of joy and thanks God because He loves them and did not create them poor beggars in the streets like the limping old man that she sees every day on her way to school and is afraid of. She imagines that God hates the poor because He did not give them anything, but she wonders why God hates the poor. And if God hates them and did not give them anything, then why does He want us to love them and give to them from what He has bestowed on us?

Her father has returned to the table to eat sweets after washing his hands from the fried meat. He hears her questions to her mother, so he tells her:

Listen, my daughter, God has a lot of wisdom in this world and He has created everything for a specific reason. He created good and evil and He created the poor and the rich. He does not hate the poor, but He created them to test the rich and see whether they are going to give to the poor or not.
Are we rich, Father?

Her father smiles and says:

We are neither rich nor poor; but thankfully, God has provided for us.
What does "provided for" mean father?
It means that what we have is enough, thank God.

Souad imagines that what they have is enough for them only and that they haven't got anything to give to the poor and that God has ordained fasting for the rich only to feel the poor people's hunger. But her father tells her that God has ordained fasting for all people, rich and poor and in the middle like them, and that every person has to give alms to the poor with whatever he can afford to pay.

But why does God order that the poor fast during the month of Ramadan when they feel hungry for the rest of the months and have no food to give to the poor?

Her father remains silent for a while and then says:

Fasting, my daughter, serves many purposes and this is God's wisdom. The rich fast to feel pain like the poor do, and the poor fast to learn more patience and to remember God. Also, because fasting is one of the pillars of Islam and it is a duty for every Muslim, just like prayer, alms giving, and pilgrimage for whoever has the means.

Souad is unable to understand her father's last words, but she knows that there are words and verses she has to learn by heart, that are not necessarily understood by the mind, because a human's mind is smaller than the mind of God and cannot comprehend all of God's wisdom. There are things she will understand when her mind grows and she becomes a grown woman like her mother.

But the most important thing that preoccupies her is that the day becomes long during the month of Ramadan, and as the heat increases her thirst increases. She feels her tongue dry inside her mouth and her lips become swollen after she runs and plays in the sun. She hears from her father that gargling with a little water does not spoil the fast provided that one does not swallow any of the water. When her mouth and tongue became very dry, she stands in front of the wash basin and fills her mouth with water and then spits it out. She repeats this a number of times. Every time, she swallows a bit of water and air and pretends that she forgot she was fasting or that the muscles of her mouth contracted involuntarily and she spits out the rest of the water as she repeats:

May God forgive me.

One day before sunset, she sees her mother in the kitchen and catches her put something in her mouth and swallow it. She realizes that her mother is deceiving God as she herself deceives Him. She feels some comfort and does not reveal her mother's secret to anyone. But that night, her mother hits her because she did not listen to her and did not wash her feet before going to bed. She sleeps and decides to reveal her secret to her father the following morning. But her father tells her that her mother does not fast for a couple of days during the month because of a specific illness. Souad is frightened and imagines that her mother is ill and will die, but her father calms her down and tells her that this condition attacks all women and girls after a certain age. She wonders if her granny and both her aunts also suffer from this disease and her father tells her:

Of course.

Then she asks:

Do I, too, get it?

Her father said that she is still young, but after a number of years the disease will affect her every month like all women. She is horrified and asks:

Do men get infected? Will my brother get infected when he grows up?

Her father assures her that he will not get infected when he becomes older because he is a boy and not a girl.

Souad feels sad and envies her brother because he was created a boy and not a girl. She feels that God loves him more than her because He does not infect him with this disease when he grows older. She does not know what the disease is, but she imagines that it is not an easy disease like a common cold that often affects her, but a disease of some mysterious kind. This mystery makes her feel that it is a dangerous secret. Her mind remains disturbed searching for the secret until she finds it out from her school friend Samira. She starts to notice at times the spots of blood on her mother's clothes from behind. But she still cannot understand the secret of this disease that makes her mother bleed and not fast or pray.

* * *

Her father teaches her the ritual ablution and prayer. She starts to perform the ablution five times a day and prays five times a day: morning, midday, afternoon, sunset, and evening. She learns the number of prostrations for every prayer and the total number of prostrations a day, which is seventeen. During the ablution she washes her face three times, gargles three times, and washes her arms, legs, and feet three times, repeating three times as she washes each part the phrase:

I ask the forgiveness of God Almighty for every great sin.

Souad practices praying. She starts her prayer with the phrase:

I invoke God's name against the accursed Satan.

Then, she reads the opening chapter of the Koran and one of the Koranic verses that she has learned, like:

I seek refuge with the Lord of the people or *Say that God is One.*

Then, she bends down to the front without bending her knees, and then she straightens her back and raises her arms until her hands are level with her head and says:

God is great.

Then, she lowers herself, bending her knees and kneeling until she touches the floor with her forehead as she says:

God listens to the one who praises Him and is grateful.

Then, she raises her head from the ground but remains kneeling and reads one of the verses, and then rises up and repeats the prostration according to every prayer. Before she ends her prayer as she kneels, she turns to the right and says:

God's peace and mercy be upon you.

Then, she turns to the left and says:

God's peace and mercy be upon you.

She does not yet understand the meaning of the words she repeats, but she has learned them by heart. She knows from her father that as she prays she stands between God's hands and she has to feel reverence and lower her head, placing her hands on her chest. She also has to expel Satan from her mind so he does not whisper anything to her during prayer, because Satan accompanies a human being like his shadow and has to be expelled when one stands between the hands of God. A human being cannot be with Satan and God at the same time because the voice of Satan might distract one's mind away from the voice of God. During prayer, humans have to empty their minds completely for the sake of Almighty God to hear His voice and feel His presence and the presence of the angels around Him—in particular, the two angels who stand to her right and to her left. They stand there to protect her during prayer from Satan and other evil spirits. She has to bid them goodbye at the end of every prayer by turning toward each of them saying:

God's peace and mercy be upon you.

Souad listens to her father speak about God. Her father's voice when he speaks about God becomes soft, solemn, and inspiring, filling her heart with awe. When she starts to pray and says:

I invoke God's name against the accursed Satan.

She does not know if Satan has been expelled, so she repeats it a number of times to assure herself that she has expelled him and has no trace left. A shiver runs through her body when she imagines that God is standing in front of her and that His voice might reach her. She imagines as she kneels down that some voice is whispering to her and she shivers with fear because she does not know whether it is the voice of God or that of Satan, still following her like her shadow.

She remains perplexed, not knowing how to differentiate between the voice of God and the voice of Satan. One day she asks her father and he tells her that the voice of God orders her to be obedient and the voice of Satan orders her not to be obedient, and that a person who obeys his parents goes to Heaven and a person who obeys Satan burns in Hell fire. He also says that God observes a human and sees him every moment of the day and night, and that a human cannot lie to God because God knows everything and no one can hide anything from him.

Her fear increases after this idea, because she knows that she hides many things from God. She used to think that God cannot see her and no one sees her, but now she doesn't know what to do. She doesn't know what God will do to her because of what has passed and because of the many sins she has committed. She only committed these sins because she thought that when she is alone that she is really on her own, and that no one can see her when she is in her locked room, or when she goes to class and opens Mohammed's schoolbag to eat the cake before anyone comes in, or when she hides her hand with the pumpkin seeds without the buyer seeing her, or when she hides under the bed with her sister and brother to play, or when she swallows some of the water before it is sunset in the month of Ramadan.

But she now realizes that she is never alone, and that God sees her every minute, and He saw her every time she ate Mohammed's cake, and He saw her when she filled her hand with pumpkin seeds, and He saw her every time under the bed, and He saw her when she swallowed the water before sunset.

But her mind for quite some time remains unable to believe that when she is alone she is not alone, and that other eyes see her although she does not see them. She does not understand how those eyes could penetrate the ceiling, walls, and door to reach her as she sits alone in her room or under the bed. Could God be like the evil spirits and ghosts that come in through the gaps in the window or the cracks in the door? She imagines for the first time that God saw her when she stole the pumpkin seeds because she was standing in the street near the cart and no ceiling covered her from the sky. God in the sky could have easily seen her. But many questions cross her mind: How can God stand in the sky? Does He actually stand or sit? Either way, He cannot look at the ground. He would have to lie down so that His face is directed below to see the ground and watch people as they walk in the streets or stand beside the pumpkin seed cart. How could He watch all the enormous numbers of people in all the long, wide, and limitless streets? She imagines that God did not see her when she stole the pumpkin seeds or because there are other pumpkin seed carts in the other streets she might have been lucky and God's eyes were directed to another cart the moment she filled her hands with pumpkin seeds.

But all these questions have no answer in her brain. She starts to fear that God can see her as she enters the toilet and locks the door. She becomes embarrassed when she takes off her underwear to pee, and imagines God's eyes watching her. She even imagines that God is standing behind her and she can feel his breath on the back of her neck. A shiver runs through her body and she looks behind quickly, imagining she will find a person behind her; but she finds no one. She asks her father once more how God could squeeze through the walls and door. He tells her that God is only a spirit and has no body, while a human has a body and spirit. She imagines that a human possesses more things than God because God is only a spirit, but a human has a spirit and a body. But her father orders her to ask for God's forgiveness three times because God owns the heavens and earth and the whole of the universe, including the people. As for humans, they are one of God's creatures and do not own anything. They do not even possess their own life because God can order their death any minute He desires.

Every time she hears her father speak about God, she becomes more scared and her sense of guilt increases. God has seen her commit all these previous sins and no doubt she is going to Hell, and she will not escape God's punishment no matter what she does and no matter how much she prays or fasts. God has seen her and the matter is over. She cannot deceive God with her kneeling and praying because God knows that she is guilty and deserves to be punished, and He will punish her whether she prayed or not. This hopeless feeling gives her a great sense of relief as she stops praying for a number of days and forgets a lot of what her father told her. Her heart feels lighter after the feelings of fear and guilt no longer accompany her. She starts to give in once more to the pleasures of the things she loves, but she continues to feel guilty when she reaches out and fills her hand with pumpkin seeds. She feels that God can see her when she goes under the bed, but the guilty feeling soon disappears and she imagines that God does not see her. Her mind is still unable to imagine how God could see her. She has no more hope of going to Heaven, no matter what she does. The afterlife seems so far away and her death is far away or impossible. Her mind cannot yet comprehend that she might die.

Her father notices that she no longer prays or fasts, and he asks her the reason. She is unable to tell him that she has committed many sins and that God has seen her and will punish her. She tells him that she does not pray because she doesn't know how to expel Satan, and that she cannot distinguish between the voice of God and the voice of Satan, and that she feels guilty and will go to Hell and her prayers will not be of benefit. Her father tells her that she is still young and that she has not yet committed any dangerous sins, and that all people make mistakes, and that a human by nature errs and is drawn toward evil and sins. But God forgives the sins of those who pray and ask forgiveness. God has created prayer to give a human the chance to ask for God's forgives and God is forgiving and merciful.

Souad felt comfortable and continued praying. Every time she performed the ablution she would raise her voice high and repeat:

I ask the forgiveness of God Almighty from every great sin.

At the beginning of prayer she would repeat:

I invoke God's name against the accursed Satan.

And a shiver would run through her body when her mind would picture that Satan still accompanies her and that she will not be able to distinguish between the voice of Satan and the voice of God. But she starts to realize that Satan's voice is that which whispers to her with the pleasurable things she loves, like stealing pumpkin seeds, or playing that game under the bed, or gulping Mohammed's cake, or drinking water before it is time for *Iftar*. She imagines that every time she feels some sort of pleasure, that it is evidence that she has carried out Satan's order and not an order from God. But her guilt feeling soon disappears after she prays and asks for God's forgiveness.

One day during dinner, her mother gave her half a stuffed pigeon. She loves stuffed pigeons more than any other food in the world. She feels hungry and eats her food with great speed. But suddenly she remembers Satan and imagines that it was he who induced her to feel this pleasure. She leaves the kitchen and gives half her pigeon to Fathiya. This is the first time in her life she has been able to resist the pleasure that Satan whispers to her, and the first time she has been able to give Fathiya something God has given her.

She is unable to hide the news of the victory from her father. But her father tells her that God did not say she should give her food to the servant, because servants have their own food that God provides them with, and the masters of the house have theirs. He tells her that the pleasure of food is not forbidden. She asks him about the forbidden pleasures so she can resist them. Her father becomes silent for a while and then tells her that she will get to know these things when she grows up and that the pleasure of food is not among the forbidden pleasures.

From that day on, she starts to eat with freedom and gluttony, too, for she realizes that the pleasure of food is allowed. She practices it without feeling the guilt that accompanies her when she feels other pleasures.

*   *   *

Souad continues to feel this overwhelming pleasure when she rides the train and senses its swift movement as it rushes forward. It whistles and puffs out thick smoke, and its wheels creak against the rails. The lampposts run backwards at a maddening speed. She jumps in her seat from joy, imagining that they are traveling to her granny's house in Kafr Al Bagour or to her grandfather's house in Al

Abbasiyah; but her father has been transported from Alexandria to another town called Desouk.

For the first time her mind picks up these names: Kafr Al Bagour, Al Abbasiyah, Alexandria, and Desouk. She asks her mother:

Does Desouk have a sea like Alexandria?

Her mother tells her:

Desouk doesn't have a sea but it has a Nile like the Nile in Kafr Al Bagour and has fields and beautiful clean houses, not like the houses in Kafr Al Bagour.

Souad is happy with her new room in the new house. It has a big window with metal railings, but it overlooks a big field where the sun shines on the golden spikes of wheat and is surrounded by thick trees with hovering birds. White pigeons stand on the low roofs of the houses and ducks swim in the small canal next to the field.

In the field, there is a boy called Sabry who wears a long *galabiya* with red and white stripes. He rolls his *galabiya* up to his waist then wades into the canal and makes a big opening in the mud with his hands for the water to rush from the canal to the field and water the plants. Sometimes he holds a small pickaxe and hits the ground hard with it.

Souad starts to go to the field and watch Sabry as he moves his arms powerfully and hits the ground with the pickaxe. She asks him to give her the pickaxe to dig the ground like him. Sabry laughs and tells her that she wears a dress and shoes and cannot dig the ground in a dress and shoes. Souad quickly takes off her shoes, rolls up her dress, takes the pickaxe from Sabry, and hits the ground.

The movement of her arms as they rise in the air and then powerfully come down gives her a peculiar sort of pleasure. The feeling of the mud under her bare feet intoxicates her body. As she chases the flying pigeons at utmost speed, she feels that she, too, is about to fly in the air. Her chest expands with fresh air. The golden wheat spikes shake and dance under the sun and nothing impedes the movement of her body. The movement reaches every cell in her body and her mind at the same time, so her whole being moves as if it is one cell with united parts in complete harmony with her arms and legs, and with the wings of the pigeons as they fly, and with the wheat spikes as they shake and dance.

The thing she loves most in Desouk is to go to the field, and the thing she hates most is to go to school and sit in class. She spends hour after hour seated at her wooden desk with her body squeezed between two wooden planks: one of them presses against her backside and the other presses against her stomach from the front, and underneath her it presses against her buttocks while her feet are raised under the seat on a wooden foot rest. The teacher stands by the blackboard pointing with his long pointed stick or walks between the rows of pupils with his stick shaking behind his back, and the tassel shakes on his tarbush. Souad tightens her lips so that she does not let out a laugh, and her body shakes with suppressed laughter so the teacher stings her on the back with the stick and says:

Sit properly and don't quiver like a spring.

In front of her sits a pupil called Mokhtara. The teacher never hits her with the stick no matter how much she laughs, but just tells her:

Don't laugh, Mokhtara, and pay attention to the lesson or I will tell your father.

Behind her sits a pupil called Fathy. He hits him more than any other pupil and always calls him:

You animal, son of an animal.

Beside her to the right sits a lame pupil called Fatima who places a crutch under her armpit when she walks, and when she sits down she places the crutch against the wall next to her. Souad never comes near the wall because she fears the strange appearance of the crutch, and it reminds her of the crutch of the old beggar who used to walk behind her as she walked in the street and she imagined that he would pounce on her from behind.

Beside her to the left sits a pupil called Michel. He smiles at her when he first sees her and asks her what her name is, and she says *Souad*. During recess, Michel gives her half his sandwich and they play together in the schoolyard and go up to class together. Souad is happy because she has another friend.

The following day, a tall girl called Zeinab comes up to her. She sits in the back row and asks what her name is, and she answers *Souad*. She asks her:

Are you a Muslim?

She says:

Yes.

She says:

Thank God, I thought you were a blue bone.

Souad does not understand what a *blue bone* is, so she tells her:

A blue bone means a Copt, and Copts are not Muslims but infidels, and infidels go to Hell because they do not believe. Their whole lives are full of one forbidden thing after another and their money is forbidden, so is their food; Michel is a Copt like them and he will go to Hell with them and his food is forbidden.

Souad feels a slight shiver run through her body, and when she turns to Michel and he smiles at her, she does not smile back. When he holds out his hand with half his sandwich, she tells him in an equivocal voice that she is not hungry. During

recess, when he asks her to play with him in the
schoolyard, she says that she does not want to play.

When Souad returns home that day she asks her
father if it is true that the Copts are infidels and will
go to Hell. Her father said:

> *Only Muslims will go to Heaven because they believe*
> *in our Master Mohammed, who is God's prophet, but*
> *the Copts don't believe in our Master Mohammed,*
> *they believe in our Master Jesus and call him the*
> *Messiah and believe that he is the son of God; and*
> *this is extreme infidelity and is punished by Hell fire*
> *because God is one who is neither begotten nor begets*
> *and has never had a partner.*

Souad starts to ask every time she gets to know a
new pupil:

> *Are you a Muslim or a Copt?*

She thanks God because the whole class has
only one Copt: Michel. She sees him sit alone in
the schoolyard and watch the other pupils play.
Sometimes the sun falls on his face and it appears
red; Souad thinks that God makes the sun change
into fire to burn Michel's face, and she is sometimes frightened by the redness of his face under
the sun and thinks that the rays will turn into fire
any minute. She moves away from him and stands
on the other side of the schoolyard where the fire
cannot reach her or where she can run before it
reaches her.

One day, Michel goes up to Souad and asks her:

Why are you upset with me, Souad?

She tells him that he is an infidel and he will go
to Hell and that she is a Muslim and will go to
Heaven, and she does not want to speak to him
because God will put her in Hell with him if she
becomes his friend. Michel tells her that he is not
an infidel and that he will go to Heaven like her
because he believes in God and in the Messiah, the
son of God. Souad says:

*God did not beget the Messiah, he did not beget
anyone.*

Michel answers:

*The Messiah is the son of God or else where did the
Messiah come from? Is it possible that someone can be
given birth to without a father?*

Souad does not know how to answer the question. She knows that a child cannot be born unless
the father and mother sleep in the same bed. She
waits until she goes back home and asks her father.
Her father tells her:

*Our Master Jesus was born to our Lady the Virgin
Mary without a father because God breathed from
his soul into her and this is one of the miracles of
God, who is able to do anything and is the one who
created human beings. He is the one who created*

the sky, earth, sun, moon, stars, and everything in the universe. He created everything in 7 days and he can destroy it all in one moment, just by ordering the sky to fall to the ground, and all the people would die.

Souad asks in astonishment:

Can the sky fall to the earth father?

Her father answers:

Of course, my daughter, and this will happen on Doomsday when God will give an order to the sun and moon and sky and they will all fall to earth and all the people will die, then they will wake up again so that God can punish them for what they did in life. They have to walk on the straight path, which is a long thread as thin as a hair, passing over fire. Heaven lies at its end.

Souad opens her mouth in astonishment and says:

How will people walk on this thin line? Will they definitely fall father?

Her father says as he rubs his hands with enthusiasm:

The ones who will fall are the infidels and disbelievers and the ones among the Muslims who did not obey God. Those will lose their balance and fall into Hell. As for the Muslims who obey God and His Prophet, they will walk easily on the straight path and their bodies will become light and they will know how to keep their balance and run along the straight path until they reach Heaven.

Souad remains amazed, her mouth open, and her mind speculates:

How can a person walk along a thin hair? Won't it break? Won't the person's body fall from it? And how can the body keep its balance?

The question imposes itself on her mind when she crosses the canal on a thin pipe much thicker than a hair's breadth. Despite this, her body sways and she almost falls into the canal but for the fact that the canal is narrow and she can jump quickly to the other side before she falls down.

One day, Souad goes with her father, sister, and brother to the circus, where a big tent is set up near the bridge, on the other side of the Nile. Souad sits beside her father watching the animal tricks with great pleasure and happiness until it is the turn of the man who walks on a tight rope between two high trees. Her eyes are fixed on the man's feet and she holds her breath as he sways on the rope. Every time the man is about to fall, Souad screams with fright. But her father reassures her and tells her the man is trained to walk on the rope and will not fall down. Souad is comforted and asks her father suddenly:

Is the straight path like this rope, Father?

Her father says:

The straight path is thinner than the rope: it is a hair's breadth.

Souad goes quiet for a while and feels that she must join the circus to train herself to walk along very thin ropes so she won't fall down from the straight path. But her father asserts that practicing will be of no help to anyone on Doomsday: what will help on that day is prayer, almsgiving, fasting, and obeying God and one's mother and father.

*   *   *

Souad often forgets about the straight path, Heaven, and Hell as she rushes to play in the field. Her pleasure as she moves her arms and legs in the air surpasses any other pleasure. It overcomes any other pleasure in her mind and makes her forget everything, including food. She does not feel hungry when her mother calls out for her from the window because it is time for dinner. She hides behind the tree and continues to run in the field and move her arms and legs in the air as she plays.

The thing she hates most is when her father calls out to her to study. She can never hide behind a tree or anything else, for she fears her father more than her mother. Her mother's hand never hurts her no matter how hard she hits her, and her eyes, when she gets angry with her, do not become a frightful red, as happens with her father, who makes his eyes seem the eyes of another man she does not know. She moves back away from him and sticks to her mother. Her mother is always her mother no matter what mistakes she makes; even if she does not listen to her, she remains her mother. When she fails her midyear exam, her father locks her up in her room without lunch or dinner, and her mother brings her food in her room and pats her before she goes to sleep. Souad puts her arms around her mother and says:

I love you, Mama.

Her mother says to her:

And I love you, Souad.

She says:

But my father doesn't love me.

She tells her:

Your father loves you, Souad, but when you play and you don't study and fail in the exam, he doesn't love you as he wants you to succeed.

Souad says:

But mama, you love me whether I fail or succeed.

Her mother kisses her as she says:

I love you whether you fail or succeed, but I love you more when you succeed.

Souad says:

But I don't like to study and I don't like school.

Her mother asks her:

Why don't you like school and studying, Souad?

Souad tightens her lips in silence. She doesn't know why she hates school and hates to study. All that she knows is that she hates to sit all these hours without movement, and hates the words she memorizes and repeats in front of the teacher without understanding anything. If she forgets a phrase or makes a single mistake, the teacher stings her hand with the stick and tells her:

You're an ass.

But he would not hit Mokhtara and does not call her an ass, no matter how much she forgets or makes mistakes. She did not know why the teacher does not hit her like he hits other pupils, until her classmate Fatima told her that Mokhtara is the sheriff's daughter, and all the people in Desouk fear the sheriff and have a lot of consideration for him.

Souad asks her mother about the sheriff and whether the sheriff is better than her father, and why people fear the sheriff but do not fear her father. Her mother says that people fear the sheriff because he can put them in prison and he has many soldiers, but her father does not have any soldiers.

Souad closes her eyes to sleep and dreams that her father has become a sheriff and has many soldiers who carry guns and people fear him. She imagines that in class, the teacher smiles at her and pats her on the back as he does with Mokhtara, and he does not hit her and call her an ass.

In the morning, her father comes to her bedroom and pats her on her back and tells her that she has a new chance to study to not fail at the end of the year. He says he will buy her a beautiful present if she succeeds. Souad puts her arms around her father and tells him:

I love you, Baba.

Her father replies as he pats her:

And I love you, too, Souad, but I will not love you if you fail another time.

Her father performs his ablution to pray. Souad has forgotten to pray; her father reminds her and tells her that God will be content with her and will make her succeed if she prays and obeys him, and that obeying parents is part of obeying God.

Souad starts to pray regularly once more, and she starts to lock herself in her room and sit at her small desk and memorize her lessons. But the minute she hears the sound of other children beneath her window, she jumps up and runs to play with them in the field.

She enjoys the movement of her body as she runs, and even more she enjoys grabbing the pickaxe and raising it high in the air and then hitting the ground forcefully with it. It gives her immense pleasure when those little buds she buried in the soil and watered spring out from the ground, green and soft, and she feels them with her fingertips. Each day she watches them grow, and their green leaves shine in the sunlight and shake as if they are dancing. She digs her hands in the mud of the canal to make an opening for the water to flow and water the green plants. Sabry's father sees her and says to her:

> *Miss Souad, your clothes are covered in mud, your father will be angry with you and beat you. Go, my child, and study your lessons. Leave this dirty work to us the peasants.*

Souad says that she loves this kind of work more than studying. Sabry tells her that he wishes he could leave the work in the field and go to school and be able to read and write to become a respectable employee instead of a poor peasant. Souad tells him that she envies him because he does not go to school, and no one calls him an ass, and no one locks him up in the classroom. He runs all day in the wide field with the pigeons and birds, moving his arms and legs in the sun and filling his chest with fresh air. Sabry tells her that he is ready to exchange his life with hers so he would have for a father her father, the employee, and live in a clean house, sleep in a bed with blankets, eat eggs and chicken, and go to school wearing shoes and a uniform, while Souad would go live in the mud house by the edge of the Nile, sleep on the floor, and eat sharp, mature cheese. Her father would be his peasant father who walks barefoot and wears a torn *galabiya* and a worn out cap.

Souad cannot imagine her father being a poor peasant. She imagines him a sheriff, a minister, or even a king. But she hates school and hates it when her father locks her in her room to study, and she loves the field and digging the ground with the pickaxe. She loves to move her arms and legs and run on the wide, wide ground.

One day she goes with Sabry to visit their mud house by the edge of the Nile. She sees his mother with her long black dress with spots of mud, and his younger siblings with their bare thighs covered in mud and their noses and eyes dripping and covered with flies. The house is not a typical house with rooms, but one big room with a roof made out of mud and bamboo and an earth floor. Sabry points at a corner in the room and says to Souad:

I sleep here and cover with this zekeba in winter.

Souad does not know what *zekeba* is, but she sees an empty sack made out of jute. Sabry shakes the dust off it and places it on the ground, saying:

Here you are, Souad, sit down.

His mother says as she dries her brown calloused hands on her dress and wipes the sweat off her long, thin face:

Welcome, Miss Souad.

Before Souad goes to sleep that night, her mother sits next to her and pats her with her plump, white hand, her soft white body in a silk night gown. She is in her warm bed lying under woolen blankets and she thanks God He did not put her in Sabry's place. She has forgotten, as she drifts between sleep and wakefulness, her school, her studies, the exam, and everything.

The minute the sun rises, she sees the green plants shine under its golden rays as if they are dancing. As the pigeons flutter their wings in the air, she glimpses Sabry from the window in his rolled up *galabiya*, hitting the ground with the pickaxe, or watering the plants and moving his hands in the water of the canal, or running after the pigeons as he moves his arms and legs in the air. She fidgets as she sits at her desk to study. She feels her body crammed between the chair and the desk as the wood presses against her stomach from the front and her backside from behind. Her feet and legs do not move; they are fixed under the desk as if they were in metal chains. Nothing moves in her body. Her mind also does not move. Her eyes are fixed on the numbers or the words. She is memorizing their shape and making tails for them and binding them together so they will be easier to memorize. They seem to her to be separate numbers and words with nothing to bind them together but incomprehensible principles. There are typographies in the east, north, south, and west, and incidents that took place centuries ago in countries she does not know, and kings, invasions, and battles that have neither beginning nor end. Grammar rules, invariables, passive verbs, the feminine, and the uncountable.

Her father has brought her a private teacher at home who shakes his head as he reads out the grammatical rules, as if he were reciting the Koran. His tongue is heavy and he closes and opens his eyes, then closes them and opens them as he repeats:

Hhhhhhhhave you understood?

Souad says:

No.

The teacher blinks and says:

It is not important you understand; just memorize it!

At school, the teacher stands beside the blackboard with the long, pointed cane in his hand, or passes among the rows and stings the pupils on their backs, saying:

You boy there, be attentive; you girl there, pay attention.

Souad's ears pick up the teacher's voice as he speaks about a country called China and the Chinese who built a great wall around China and grow silk worms to make silk cocoons. She remembers the silk worms she often buys and places in a cardboard box with some mulberry leaves. She makes holes in the box for the air to enter so the worms won't die. The worms crawl around inside the box and climb to the edge attempting to get out, but Souad shakes the box and they fall inside to the bottom.

The teacher suddenly stings her back and asks her:

Why did the Chinese build the Great Wall around China?

Souad stands up straight and says:

So the worms will not escape to another country.

The teacher stings her a couple more times.

It is the final year exam and Souad does not pass. Her father hits her and locks her in her room for 2 days without food. She sits at her desk with the copybooks and textbooks in front of her. But her eyes escape far away and slip out through the window to the field. By the edge of the canal, she sees Sabry watering the plants with his father and laughing. She envies Sabry because his father laughs with him and does not beat him or lock him up. She has forgotten for that moment Sabry's mud house and his mother and siblings. She wishes that Sabry would give her his father and the pickaxe and field, and take her copybooks and textbooks, her desk, and her father, too.

Before Souad goes to sleep, her mother does not come to pat her to sleep and does not bring her any food. She goes to sleep hungry and dreams that her father is dead and that her mother is crying, and that she is trying to cry but cannot. She is trying to move but her feet are fixed to the ground. She is alone in a wide and dark street. She tries to run but her feet are transfixed, and suddenly she sees that long shadow. His eyes are red and bear evil. She screams but her voice does not come out.

She suddenly opens her eyes and sees her mother beside her and asks her in fright:

Where is my father?

She informs her that he is sleeping in his bedroom. She thanks God that he did not die and that she was dreaming. Then, she closes her eyes and sleeps once more.

At school, Souad finds herself back in the old classroom, but new, younger pupils are with her. She suddenly feels that her body is bigger and taller and she starts to stoop a little as she walks in line so that no one will notice that she is the biggest in her class. In class, the teacher makes her sit in the back row with the pupils who have failed. He calls that row *the failures' row*. The minute one of them makes a mistake in one of the sentences or forgets a word, the teacher's cane stings him and the words *you failure* ring in her ears.

Souad's hatred of school, classes, and studying increases. It is connected in her mind with a sort of humiliation and disappointment because of her tall frame. She looks at herself in the mirror and hates her big body and wishes she was as small as Fatima, who also failed but is small in stature so no one can distinguish her from the new pupils. She plays with them on the playground as if she were one of them.

But Souad stands alone in the playground. She is ashamed to play with the small pupils in her class. She plays more with some of her old friends, including football with Mokhtara, the sheriff's daughter.

She feels proud when she plays football with Mokhtara, and she often sits and chats with her after school on the wooden bench. Samira, a friend of Mokhtara's, sometimes joins them. The car horn sounds in the air and Samira leaves them to ride in the red car next to her father who is a physician. Seconds later the soldier, who carries Mokhtara's schoolbag, appears and takes her home in the police car. Souad returns home on foot, carrying her schoolbag in her hand and feeling that her father is poor, with no car and no soldiers.

She wonders as she walks why God has given a car and soldiers to the sheriff and not to her father. Does God love the Sheriff more than He loves her father? Even though her father obeys God and prays a lot and fasts? And she also prays and fasts, and her mother also prays and fasts the whole month of Ramadan, except for those few days in which she becomes ill. She is overcome by a strange feeling of anger toward God. She feels that He does not love her father enough or prefers the sheriff to him and the physician. She also feels that God loves Mokhtara more than her because

He made her the sheriff's daughter, and Samira more than her because He made her the physician's daughter.

Souad stamps on the ground in anger as she walks under the burning sun. Her fingers are swollen from the weight of the copybooks and textbooks in the schoolbag. She imagines Mokhtara seated in the car and the soldier carrying her schoolbag for her. But this anger soon disappears when she sees her friend Fatima as she swings on her wooden crutches. She pants as she limps with her slow, heavy steps, with sweat pouring from her forehead. Souad thanks God as she stamps the ground with her two strong feet and runs home moving her arms and legs in the air.

Mokhtara invites her to her house on her birthday. It is the first time she has attended a birthday party. Her father and mother do not celebrate anyone's birthday. The only celebration she knows is the small feast after the month of Ramadan, when her mother makes cookies, and the big feast when her father buys a sheep and the butcher comes to slaughter it at dawn.

Souad goes inside Mokhtara's house and finds that it is much better than her house. It is surrounded by a big garden and has big golden chairs; a big clock hangs on the wall and a big dining table is lit with candles and covered with various types of sweets and pastries she has neither seen nor tasted before.

Souad becomes certain that day that God loves Mokhtara more than He loves her, because He has given her all these things. She wonders if Mokhtara prays more than her. As she sits at the table beside Mokhtara, she suddenly asks her:

Mokhtara, do you fast in Ramadan?

Mokhtara tells her that she does not fast because she is still young. Souad asks her:

Do you pray?

Mokhtara says that she does not pray, but when she grows up she will learn to. At this point, Souad raises her head with some pride and says:

My father taught me how to pray and I pray every day; and I fasted last year and the year before as well.

Souad feels some sort of contentment because she has distinguished herself. Mokhtara is richer than her, but Souad has learned to pray before her. She prays and fasts and Mokhtara does not. But this feeling soon vanishes and a puzzling question occurs to her. She tells herself if she prays and fasts and Mokhtara does not, then God should favor her over Mokhtara. And if God favors her over Mokhtara, then why did He give Mokhtara more than He gave her?

The question keeps puzzling her until she returns home and tells her mother that God is unjust because He gave Mokhtara more than He gave her, although she prays and fasts and Mokhtara does not. Her mother says that she must ask for God's forgiveness, repeating three times the phrase *I ask God's forgiveness,* because God is just and He gives to whoever He wants and denies whoever He wants, as He is free to do what He wants with his worshippers. She tells her that God, be praised, has given them what suffices for them and they are not greedy. She should not be greedy and should be content with what God has given her, because God gives every human being according to what he deserves.

But Souad's brain at that moment is unable to grasp what her mother says. She cannot imagine how God could be just when He gives the one who prays to Him less than the one who does not pray to Him. If God gives to every human according to what he deserves, then God must have thought that Mokhtara deserves more things than her, that Mokhtara is better than her, that she is worth less than Mokhtara.

She is overcome by a strange feeling of humiliation, pettiness, and unworthiness. She feels that God knows her true nature because God knows everything. This feeling settles inside her and her mind is content with it. It is the only feeling that convinces her of God's justice, because if she felt that she is like Mokhtara and deserves what Mokhtara deserves, then God cannot be just, because He has not given her what He has given to Mokhtara. Because God cannot be unjust, then she must be worth less than Mokhtara and she does not deserve what Mokhtara deserves.

Her mind calms and her conscience relaxes from a feeling of guilt, for she does not want to cast doubt on God's fairness in any way. It is better to wrong herself and label herself with unworthiness than to accuse God of injustice. By wronging herself she does not feel guilty or fearful, but a strange feeling of humiliation is suppressed inside her and she does not realize it except when she goes to school and stands in line. At this moment, she lowers her head and stoops her back and remains like that until she sits in her place in the back row. There, she shrinks and curls her arms and legs into her big body in the small space between the bench behind her and the desk in front of her.

Her mother notices that she stoops as she walks, and starts to alert her to straighten her back and not to make a habit of this stooping posture or she will develop a hump like a camel's. She has seen a camel's hump and is frightened that a hump like it will grow on her back. She starts to straighten her back muscles every time she remembers her mother's words. But the minute she goes to school she bends her back without realizing. When she sits at her desk she remains stooped, and bends her head over the copybook or the textbook. Her body remains in this posture as long as she is in class or when she sits studying at the desk in her room. It appears to whoever sees her that she is studying, but she is not. Her eyes only stare at the book, but her mind is thinking of the other things she loves. She loves to run and play in the field, but she no longer goes out because her father swore not to let her go to the field, play, or waste time. He tells her that she has grown up and has become like a mule, and it would be shameful if she fails ever again.

* * *

On the train, Souad no longer jumps with joy and no longer runs to sit beside the window. But her heart still beats as she feels the rapid movement of the train, and the old pleasure runs through her body as she watches the rails retreat at amazing speed. Her mother says that they are traveling to her grandfather's house in Kafr Al Bagour, and that she will also see her grandmother and aunt and uncle in the big *dowar*. Souad does not know what the big *dowar* is. Her mother says that her father has a big house in Kafr Al Bagour, which they call the *dowar*. Her great-grandfather used to live there, Sheikh Al Bagoury. He was wealthy and had a lot of land and black slaves. But he died and left behind many children from his three wives. Her father sold his share of the land because he did not like the problems of the land and the peasants, and because he spent a lot of money on himself and his pleasure. He loved to stay out late and drink, and he visited Kafr Al Bagour only once after the death of his father. This is the second time and it is not a visit to his relatives the peasants, but migration from Cairo to the village because there is war in Cairo. The bombs are falling from the sky on the houses and are destroying them and burning them.

Souad listens attentively to her mother's voice and picks out for the first time new words she has not heard before: *war, bombs falling from the sky*. Her eyes widen in amazement and look at the sky in dread. How can the sky drop bombs? Who throws them? Is it God, since He is the only one who lives in the sky? Why does God destroy the houses and burn them? Is He punishing the people like Mokhtara, who did not obey Him and did not pray or fast? Or is He punishing her grandfather because he loves to stay out late and drink alcohol, and drinking alcohol is forbidden, as she heard from her father? Or is God destroying the houses because Doomsday has come and all people will die and she will die and her father, mother, brother, and sister will all die? Her eyes move to her mother with a strange sort of fear, bewilderment, and wonder. Why is God punishing them just as he is punishing the others who do not pray or fast even though she prays and fasts, and her father prays and fasts, and her mother ... but her mother tells her that God is not dropping bombs on people and houses, the airplanes of the enemies are. The word *enemies* rings in her ears and she immediately remembers the word *English* and says:

The English are our enemies.

Her father joins the conversation and tells her:

The English are our enemies Souad, but we are helping them now in their war against the Germans and the German planes are the ones that are dropping bombs on Egypt.

Souad does not understand a word her father says. How can the English be our enemies but we are helping them? Why are the Germans dropping bombs on us? Are they also our enemies? Her father says that the Germans and the English are our enemies but that we hate the Germans more than the English. We are helping the English against the Germans. After we expel the Germans, we will expel the English and become a free country that does not have any enemies inside it.

Souad closes her lips in silence, trying to gulp down the feeling of fear coming from deep inside her. The world around her seems awful and mysterious and full of enemies: English, Germans, ghosts, thieves, and djinns that come out from the heart of the sea. The sky also appears dreadful and mysterious. Her eyes fail to reach its depth and her mind is unable to imagine God. How could He sit or sleep in the sky and remain suspended like this in the air all night and day? What happens if a German plane crashes into God in the sky? Or if one of the bombs explodes in the atmosphere and burns God? Will God die? If He dies, will she continue to pray and go to school? Or will Doomsday come and will all people die, including pupils and teachers, and will there no longer be school, classes, exams, failing, or anything?

Her chest heaves as if her heart is beating fast. There is a mixture of fear and joy, but her joy is stronger than her fear and her fear is as mysterious as death. Death is further away than her mind can conceive or imagine, but school, classes, and exams feature in her mind like a part of her, like her mind itself. They do not leave her day or night. In the morning, she sits and studies without understanding, and at night she sits with an exam without answering. Death is, in her mind, mysterious and far away, or rather impossible. But the exam is near and the school is near, only a couple of steps away from home. Her heart beats with joy as she imagines a bomb falling from the sky on the school and demolishing it and burning it, burning all the wooden desks and the books, copybooks, and exam questions.

She jumps from her seat as she hears a sound like an explosion. But it is not a bomb. It is a car's horn blowing, and the children scream as they ride on the back of the car and surround it from every direction singing out:

Hassan Bey, Oh, Hassan Bey.

Amid their faces covered with flies, she glimpses the face of her cousin Zaki. She smiles at him and Zaki runs with his bare feet and reaches out with his hand through the car window and holds her father's hand and kisses it as his voice shouts in rejoice:

The whole world is shining, Uncle. Thank God for your safe arrival!

The car stops in front of her grandfather's mud house. From the nearby mud houses, men in *galabiyas* and women with black scarves come out and look at the car with wide-open eyes and open mouths. They see a car only once or twice every year when a big official like Hassan Bey Abu Zeid comes to Kafr Al Bagour.

The alley gets crowded with men, women, aunts, uncles, nieces, nephews, all shouting:

> *A thousand welcomes, a thousand welcomes. The village is shining, the whole world is shining.*

Men's voices mix with the women's and children's, and the dust rises with their voices in the air.

Hajja Amna must have heard the car horn and her ears picked up her son's name *Hassan Bey,* so she goes out to the street. She walks among the crowds with her tall, thin stature and the voices around her shout to make room for the Bey's mother. She straightens her back with pride and raises her head above the others. Her small eyes devoid of eyelashes widen and search for her son. She singles him out from the rest and with open arms rushes toward him. The minute he gets out of the car she receives him into her arms and kisses him all over. She kisses his face, head, *tarbush,* his neck, and smells him. It is the smell of her only son: one son among six daughters. His father left when he was young and she was the one who taught him. She worked hard and went hungry to educate him. Her dream has become a reality, and here he is in flesh and blood in his suit and *tarbush.* He comes to the village in a car, not on a donkey's back, with his three children around him (*God be praised!*) and his wife the madam, daughter of the great Bey.

It is Souad's turn to be hugged by her grand-mother, after her father and mother. Her granny places her long, veined arms around her chest and kisses her several times as she squeezes her. Souad is suffocated by her grandmother's breath mixed with the smell of dust, sweat, milk, cream, and pastries. She slips away from her and is received by one aunt after another who kiss her and says:

> *God be praised, God be praised. The whole world is shining, Hassan Bey, the whole world is shining, Miss Souad.*

She feels suffocated by their breath and the smell of dust, sweat, and pastry; but her grandmother's joy and her aunts' stir her heart as she stands among her barefoot cousins with her shiny leather shoes and her silk dress. She feels that she is Miss Souad and that her father is a real Bey. She walks beside her father, holding his hand and thanking God that He made her the daughter of her father and not the daughter of the peasant Abdullah, Zaki's father.

But this pride does not last for long when Souad goes with her mother and father to her grandfa-ther's *dowar*, and her father is instantly demoted from *Hassan Bey* to *Hassan Effendi* and she is demoted from *Miss Souad* to *Souad* or *the girl Souad*. Her grandfather's house is spacious, with many rooms; its floor is not made of earth and it is covered with carpet rather than straw matting. The bedrooms have beds and wardrobes, and the bathrooms have taps and water. Her grandfather sits in the spacious hall wearing silk pajamas and her grandmother sits silent, neither kissing her nor talking to her. Her aunt does not hug or kiss her, but she embraces her mother. Her uncle shakes her hand with his plump white palm and says *Hello, Souad*, and then he sits to speak with her father and grandfather.

Souad remains seated in a corner of the hall, her eyes move from her grandfather to her uncle to her father. Her father is wearing the white *galabiya* he slept in. He appears in his *galabiya* like a poor peasant beside her grandfather and uncle. No one here is happy with their coming and no one says that the world is shining.

She hears her grandfather speak of the war and bombs, and her uncle says that he hates the English and loves the Germans. Her father says that he hates the English and hates the Germans. Her uncle says that the Germans are better than the English, and that the king is with the Germans and wants them to win the war. Her father says that the king is not working for the good of the country, and that Al Nahhas works for the sake of the country. Her aunt comes and says that she loves the king because he is good-looking. She says she does not love Al Nahhas because she does not like the look of his eyes because one of his eyes does not look straight like the other one, and he seems, to her, to be looking with only one eye in his pictures.

Souad does not know yet who Al Nahhas is, but she wants to go to her grandmother's house where her cousins are. Her mother tells her to stay at her grandfather's house so she can sleep in a comfortable, clean bed. At her grandmother's house, she will sleep on a straw mat and fleas will bite her all night long. But Souad tells her mother that she doesn't want to stay at her grandfather's house and wants to go to her grandmother's and sleep on the straw mat, and go to the field with her cousin Zaki, and eat the hot pastries that her grandmother bakes in the oven. Her aunt hears her and tells her:

You're a peasant.

She is overcome by an old feeling of shame and she feels that the word *peasant* is a kind of insult or humiliation.

*   *   *

Her grandmother Hajja Amna squats on the floor in the courtyard, and in front of her is a straw mat covered with wheat. Its yellow seeds shine in the sun. Her grandmother reaches out and fills her palm with wheat grains, then brings them up close to her eyes to spot the small, black stones, singles them out with her index finger and thumb, and throws them away on the ground one after another.

As Souad sits beside her, she follows the movement of her fingers. Her fingers are like her father's, long and dark, but her flesh is wrinkled and her veins protrude like thin snakes. Her wide black dress is fastened at the neck with a red button. Nothing of her but her big cracked feet appear from under the dress as she squats. Her big toe resembles her father's: it is long and thick, but the other toes are short and curled.

She imitates her, filling her palm with wheat, then picking out the black stones and throwing them away. She competes with her grandmother: she sees the stones quicker and throws four or five of them away in the time it takes her grandmother to throw away just one. It is a nice game that appeals to her. The grains of wheat dance golden in the sunlight; the birds swoop and chirp and race to pick a grain of wheat with their beaks. Her grandmother's low voice reaches her ears as she talks and talks nonstop:

When your father was young he was like you. He used to love sitting with me and help me pick the wheat. I used to tell him, get up, my son, and study your lessons so you will pass and succeed, and he used to say that he has passed and succeeded and that he is the second in his class. I used to tell him: And why aren't you the first? Is the first one better than you? Didn't a woman like your mother give birth to him? And in the whole village there is no woman like your mother. She works in the field and in the house and is worth ten men. Your grandfather died when he was a young man and left me one boy and six girls. He left us nothing but this house and this barren little plot. Everyone told me: Amena, let your son become a peasant like his father. Let him hold the axe and take over the field work from you. But I said: There is no way that my son would become a peasant. Isn't it enough that his father died before his time because he stood all day under the sun? I told myself: Amena, as long as you're alive and have a breath in you, your son will never hold an axe. Send him to Cairo to get educated and work and become a respectable Effendi like Ibrahim Effendi, the son of your neighbor Hosniya. Is Hosniya better than you, Amena? She is a lonely woman like you without a man or land or support. She sold her gold necklace and anklet and educated her son in Cairo. He is now wearing a suit and tarbush and comes to the village in a car with a horn, and everyone points at him and says: Ibrahim Effendi, Hosniya's son.

Her eyes continue watching the shining golden grains, and the wings of fluttering birds under the sun, and the movement of the long index finger with the veins, and the thick and wrinkled thumb as they pick one pebble after another. Her grandmother's low voice continues nonstop like her breath as she blows away the straw from the wheat that fills her palm. Her lips are full of lines and wrinkles and her nose is long and snubbed like her father's. Her narrow eyes without eyelashes look at her and fill her eyes with her white round face like her mother's and her wide black eyes like her father's. Her small hands play with the wheat grains and throw them to the birds and her ears listen to her grandmother's voice, which is as slow as her breathing. She knows the words and has learned them by heart as she repeats them every day without pause and without getting tired or bored. The minute she comes to an end, she starts all over again, like a reel of thread going round and round. The reel never ends, the thread is never cut, and the grains of wheat on the straw mat never finish. Her grandmother's fingers do not stop moving like her lips as she blows the straw and the words together:

Your father was quiet and obedient. I used to tell him: Study, my son, so that God will help you succeed and prevent you from living like the peasants, so that you will have something in this world and have a house and get married to a woman from the city whose father is a Bey, so that your sisters will thrive with your presence. If one of them gets angry with her husband or her husband divorces her she will find a place in your house.

She never sees her grandmother except sitting in the courtyard picking wheat and telling the story to her, or to herself if she is not sitting beside her. She hears her speak to herself in the same way she speaks to her, and sometimes sing to herself in a low voice and move her head and say:

I am thirsty young women, show me where the water is.

Or make a fist and wave it in the air and sing:

Oh dear, oh dear, may a catastrophe befall the English.

Souad laughs and asks her:

Have you seen the English, Granny?

She answers her:

I have not seen them, my daughter, but your father saw them and struck at them in the 1919 revolution

*with bricks and stones and they fired bullets at him.
May God strike their hearts. Your father, God bless
him, ran away from them and came to the village on
a horse-cart. He did not go back to Cairo except after
they released Saad Zaghloul from prison, and your
father made a promise that the first son he has will be
called Saad.*

After a couple of days, her grandmother
stopped talking and singing. She sat silent, looking at the sky with wandering eyes, sucking her
dry lips. Then, she stopped leaving her room and
going to the courtyard and stopped picking the
wheat. She saw her through the door lying on the
straw mat with eyes open and a gaping mouth.
Her lips were moving as if she were talking to
someone. Her father told her that her granny is
ill and wants to see her. But a strange shiver over-
came her body and she started to feel afraid to go
near her room. She imagined that she is not asleep
but dead, and that her ghost will appear in the
night.

The night in Kafr Al Bagour is scary and dark,
and there is no electric light like the ones in her
grandfather's *dowar*. There was only a small lamp
with a long flame that fills the dark walls of the
room with the shadows of ghosts and spirits.
Black insects like dung beetles crawl on the wall,
the frogs croak, mosquitoes drone, and cicadas
sing like piercing whistles. Bats come through the
windows and hit the walls. Her Aunt Khadija tells
her to hide her face with her hands, because the

bats are blind and sometimes stick to a person's face.

She hears her mother scream if she sees a cockroach run, while her aunt silently laughs and hides her mouth with her scarf and says:

City girls fear cockroaches although they neither bite nor sting like snakes.

Souad has never seen a snake, but her cousin Zaki, the son of her Aunt Khadija, tells her that a snake is long and its tail is as thin as a whip. It crawls on its stomach with its mouth open, and its breath sounds at night like a soft whistle.

That night, Souad suddenly woke up startled, as she heard a faint whistling sound. She stared in the dark, frightened, and saw a big cockroach crawl beside her. She started to be afraid of cockroaches and screamed just like her mother screamed whenever she sees one. Her Aunt Khadija laughed when she heard her scream and hid her mouth with the tip of her scarf. She laughed silently until her eyes watered, as if she were crying. She wiped her eyes with her scarf and said:

May God protect us.

Souad asks her what she means, and her aunt explains that laughter always brings evil and she is praying to God to bring good consequences.

After this, Souad realized that her peasant relatives do not laugh, or if they do they laugh silently, because they anticipate evil from God after laughing. Laughter seems to be a kind of sin for which they deserve punishment to atone for their sin.

* * *

On the train going back to Desouk, Souad is not as joyful as usual. She loves Kafr Al Bagour despite the ghosts and fleas, and loves the peasants, her father's relatives, despite their mud-stained *galabiyas* and their dark, cracked hands. She loves her cousin Zaki, and loves riding the donkey, and going to the field, and eating barbequed maize and hot pastries the minute they come out of the oven. She hates Desouk because going back to Desouk means going back to school, and studying, and being locked in her room or at the wooden desk with her head bent over the book, and her body mummified on the chair and squashed between the back of the chair behind her and the desk in front.

Her mother comes to her with a food tray and says:

Straighten your back as you sit or you will grow a hump.

She feels her back with her hand and imagines a hump growing on her back like that of a camel's. She tells her that she wants to go out and play in the field with Sabry. She allows her to go on the condition that she returns before her father comes home.

Souad jumps from her desk and rushes to the field like a rocket, running and playing and moving her arms and legs in the air. She wants to fly like the swallows and run from home and from her father and school. But she soon spots her father coming from far away. She recognizes him from afar with his tall frame, slow walk, and the movement of his arms forward and backward as the fly whisk shakes in his right hand and his left hand remains still inside his pocket.

In one leap Souad goes inside the house, and in another leap she is in her room, sitting at her desk with her head bent over the book without movement.

Her father smiles at her when he sees her and pats her on her shoulder. He says that God will help her succeed because she keeps studying and keeps praying and obeys her father and mother and does not waste time playing.

Souad remembers that she has stopped praying, so she starts once more to pray at each allotted time. She imagines that it was God who made her fail last year because she did not pray regularly. During the last part, as she kneels in prayer, she continues to kneel for a couple of extra minutes as her father does, and repeats in a soft voice like her father:

O God, help Souad to succeed this year.

When she utters the name Souad, it seems to her that she is speaking to God about another girl called Souad who isn't her. She soon realizes it is her, but she repeats: *Please God, help Souad,* as if it were not her.

One day when she is praying to God saying:

Please God, help Souad to succeed this year.

She suddenly remembers that there are three other pupils in her class called Souad, so she immediately says:

Please God, help Souad Hassan Abu Zeid.

She fears that God might make a mistake and pass another Souad instead of her.

When she strongly fears failing the exam, she starts to speak to God as she kneels, pleading:

Please God, for the sake of the prophet don't let Souad fail again this year: it is better to let her die because death for her is more bearable than failure.

She feels her hot tears run down her face and realizes that God surely sees her and sees her tears, but she still has doubts that God, while in the sky, can see her in her room. She imagines that God might hear her because the sound can go out the open window up to the sky immediately. Her tears run down her face without a sound, so she starts to weep in a loud voice and brings her head closer to the window as she raises her hands and says:

Please God, help me to succeed.

She feels that she is deceiving God with her tears, although her desire to cry is real because she has been suppressing it for a long time, and she wants to cry and cry. But her mind realizes in a secret, cunning way that she is crying to gain God's sympathy so He will let her pass. But no one could deceive God because God uncovers everything in one's heart. A shiver passes through her body and she imagines that God will be angry with her and make her fail the exam as a punishment for deceiving Him. She asks for God's forgiveness three times and asks for His help three times against Satan. She stops her prayer and dries her tears and starts once more, this time without crying. In her final kneeling posture, she raises her hands high and says:

> Please God, help me to succeed; if you help me succeed this year, I will pray regularly and will not miss a single day and will blindly obey my mother and father.

But the minute she utters these words she shivers, because the words ring in her mind as if prayer and obedience are a bribe to God for the price of her success. Prayer is a duty and obedience is a duty, as her father says, whether she fails or succeeds. No matter what catastrophes and calamities and failures befall a human, he must never lose faith in God and must continue to worship Him and pray to Him until the end of his life.

She imagines that her prayer is not accepted, for how could she think of bribing God? How could she think that God would accept a bribe just like any person without conscience? She asks God's forgiveness three times, then stops her prayer and starts anew. She ends with a prayer in which she says:

I thank you, God, and praise you whether you make me succeed or fail.

The words continue to move in her brain and she tells herself that God is the one who passes her and He is the one who fails her, and that failure and success are decreed for her by God's will before her birth. Everything in her life is decreed by God before her life began, as her religion teacher says. She feels a sort of hopelessness as she repeats the words. She realizes that no matter how much she studies and tries, she will not pass if God decrees that she should fail. She feels some sort of comfort and submission to fate, that she is helpless and has no role or will if she fails this year. But her feeling of comfort is soon followed by fear of being punished by her father. Her fear is followed by some sort of rebellion. Why should her father punish her if God is the one who chooses that she should fail? Could she pass against God's will no matter how much she studies and no matter how much she prays and fasts and raises her hands in prayer?

This night before she went to sleep, her mind whispered to her to stop praying and asking and studying and everything, for what is the use of anything? What is the use of failing or succeeding, and what is the use of life if the end is death and she will die in the end whether she passes or fails? She closed her eyes and slept deeply in a happy state.

In the morning, the idea of death evaporates from her mind and disappears just like the darkness disappears before the rays of the sun, and she sees the desk with the books and the copybooks, and her father's voice in the hall calls her to wake up and start studying before it gets too hot.

The minute her father goes out of the house, she jumps from her desk and runs to her mother to get her permission to go out. But she no longer allows her to play. She threatens to tell her father if she goes out, and Souad remains inside the house roaming between the rooms or looking from the window, or helping her mother in the kitchen, or holding a hammer or a mallet and hammering one of the broken chairs. She holds the hammer as if it were an axe and raises it high, then brings it down with all her might on the head of the nail. She repeats the blows and moves the muscles in her arms, shoulders, neck, and back. She moves with all her force until sweat drips from her forehead. She feels a peculiar pleasure in movement and a sort of relief as if there is some buried pain in her body that does not go away except with movement, or as if there is an enormous energy stored inside her like compressed steam that presses against her chest, brain, arms, and legs. She longs to move her legs with full force and hit the ground and the wall, or move her arms with the hammer and hit her wooden desk with all her might. Sometimes she hits the desk with her fist, imagining that she can smash it, but the desk remains as it is and her hand becomes red and swollen.

Her body contains suppressed energy that yearns for action. Her mind envisions movement that does not know how to come about. Whenever a carpenter or a plumber comes to the house, she stands beside him and follows his hands with her eyes as he works. She watches how the carpenter hits the nails and saws the wood. She sometimes picks the saw and moves her hands like him, and hits the nails with him. She learns from the plumber how to undo a water tap and how to place a piece of leather inside it. She moves through the rooms of the house in search of something she can hit or undo or fix.

The thing she likes most is to watch the electrician when he comes to fix some electric wires or to repair the radio. She learns from him how the radio works, and how to change a burned-out lamp, and how to attach the wires that got severed.

One morning, her mother turns on the radio but it does not produce a sound. She loves listening to the radio, and she lays awake beside it listening to the songs of Umm Kalthoum or Al Rihani. Her mother sends the maid to fetch the electrician, but the maid returns without the electrician and says he will come in the afternoon.

A feeling comes over Souad that she can fix the radio. The minute her mother goes into the kitchen, she carries the radio to her room and opens it from the back as the electrician does. She starts to search among the wires and bulbs. Her finger moves along the thin wires with care and precision and the movement of her mind as it searches for the secret of the malfunction produces a peculiar pleasure in her body. Sweat falls from her forehead, and hour after hour passes in which she is immersed among the many wires that twist in a complicated manner. She holds each wire and follows it from beginning to end, and she tries the lamps and tests them one after another. She discovers that the sound lamp is burned-out, so she hurries to her mother with a merry face and tells her that the radio can work if she buys a new sound bulb and puts it in.

Her mother screams when she sees the radio in her room with its wires and insides out:

What have you done?! You left your studies and started playing with the radio until you ruined it!

The radio was not ruined that day. The electrician came and placed in a new sound bulb and the radio worked as it used to. But no one in the house knew this; even Souad herself did not know. She did not stand beside the electrician as he worked, but stood in front of her father in her room, her head bowed like a sinner and her father's eyes red with anger. He rebuked her because she left her studies and played with the radio.

That day, her father taught her a tough lesson. He told her that she is no longer a child to play all day and that she has to succeed this year and get her primary certificate to go to secondary school and have a higher diploma. He tells her that if she fails this year, he will deprive her of education and make her stay at home to wash the floor because he does not possess any land or money or houses or anything except his salary, and he will not live forever to take care of her expenses, that a day will come when he will die and she will not find anyone to help her. He fixes his eyes on her and says:

Can't you see that you have grown up and become like a mule? You are good for nothing except eating. I am not ready to feed mules and I still have your sister and younger brother's expenses.

Something changes in Souad after this lesson. Her father does not hit her as usual, but sits calmly looking at her. As he looks in her eyes, he seems not to be her father. She shakes as she imagines that she has lived all these years with a father who is not her father, that he does not want to feed her and she can stay in the house to wash the floor or they will throw her out and she can sleep on the pavement in the dark and the thieves and ghosts will attack her. But it is no more than a fleeting moment and the normal look returns in her father's eyes, together with that faint cloud of buried sadness that resembles a mysterious storm or suppressed kindness. When he says that a day will come when he will die, Souad is unable to look into her father's eyes. Her heart beats with suppressed love like compressed steam, and some sort of fear for her father. His cool, quiet words make her feel that he will actually die soon, that his death will become a reality. Until that time, Souad has not realized the meaning of death with her mind, but her body realizes its meaning. A shiver runs through her intestines, a desire to vomit or cry. She cannot distinguish between the desire to vomit and the desire to cry. When she wants to cry, she vomits, and when she vomits, her tears fall involuntarily. She doesn't like anyone to see her tears, particularly her younger sister. She is used to suppressing crying and swallowing her tears. The tears gather in her stomach and press against her and she vomits.

Her mother thinks the vomiting is due to a disease in her stomach because she eats the produce with its mud from the field and eats the pumpkin seeds with the outer skin on which the flies have stood. Her father takes her to the doctor and the doctor says what her mother says and gives her bitter medicine. She does not drink it; she empties the spoon into the sink instead of into her mouth. Her mother catches her once doing this, so she holds her and her father makes her drink the medicine. She closes her mouth tightly, but her father blocks her nose with his hand until she feels she will suffocate and die, so she opens her mouth wide to breathe and he pours the medicine in it.

* * *

Souad passes the exams that year and gets her primary certificate. Her mother and father are happy for her, and her father buys her a watch as a reward. Friends come to the house to congratulate them. She hears her father say that she has become an obedient daughter and her father's friends say that God will stand beside her and will always help her succeed.

Souad does not stop praying after she passes, so that God will not think that she was praying just for the sake of the exam. She continues to pray regularly, raising her hands high and saying:

Thank you, God, because you caused me to pass.

Her father calls out to her to greet the guests. Souad receives their congratulations but her heart feels heavy. A strange sensation overtakes her because she feels that the one who passed the exam was not her but God, or God's deputy in the form of an angel who descended from the sky and answered the questions or told her the answers. When her father's friends congratulate her for her success, she thinks that she does not deserve the congratulations or the present, that she doesn't deserve anything. She is overcome by feelings of humiliation and insignificance. A big tear crawls at the edge of her eye; she quickly swallows it before anyone sees it, and then smiles at her father's friends, pretending to be happy. She fears that someone might discover what is going on in her mind.

Many questions circle in her mind without answer. The question that occupies her mind at the moment is: Because God is the one who decides her success or failure, then does she deserve punishment if she fails or reward if she succeeds?

Her father tells her that God decrees failure and success and decides good and evil, but He gives the human a brain to distinguish between good and evil.

Souad wonders what the benefit is for a human to think and choose good, for example, if God has decreed evil for him? Can a human do good against God's will? Her father says that God only decrees evil for evil people, but for the good ones He decrees good. Souad says that God is the one who creates the evil and the good, so can the evil become good against God's will? Her father says that nothing in the universe can take place without God's will. She wonders why God punishes the evil if He is the one who created them evil and He is the one who decreed evil for them?

Her father's voice rises with anger as he says:

This is God's wisdom in His creation and He is free to do what He wants with His slaves. He gives to who He wants, and denies who He wants, and He bestows gifts on who He wants, and leads astray who He wants. Everything goes according to His will. He is the wise knower.

Although her father's voice rises in angry, Souad is still unable to understand. Her mind refuses to accept that the evil ones deserve to go to Hell while they have no hand in anything. Also, the good ones, similarly, do not deserve to go to Heaven because it is God who makes them good: they do not make themselves good.

Her father's voice continues to rise and the red color of anger seeps into the white of his eyes as he tells her that she has to expel the devil from her mind and spirit and she has to believe in God's wisdom because God is the one who created humans. The creator is greater than the created and the created cannot ask the creator the secret of His wisdom. It is God only who knows the secrets and she has to believe in God and His wisdom with unshakable faith. Strong faith is in the heart, not the mind, because a human's mind is unable to grasp Almighty God's power.

Souad leaves the question hanging without an answer, and she soon forgets it. She no longer thinks of it. Whenever she stands between God's hands in prayer, a shiver of fear and dread runs through her because she is unable to tell whether God has decreed for her to go to Heaven or to Hell, nor whether He is going to decree her among the good or among the evil. Sometimes she raises her hands high and asks God what He has decided for her life. She imagines that a voice whispers to her and she does not know whether it is God's voice or the devil's. Because of her fear, she does not listen to what the voice tells her and she ends the prayer quickly to get rid of her fear.

One day, she sees her mother crying in a muffled voice and wearing a black dress. She finds out that her grandfather has died, and she imagines that he died because he drank a lot of alcohol and that he will go to Hell. But her mother tells her that he drank alcohol in his youth and then asked for God's forgiveness. He used to pray at the end of his days and he will go to Heaven. Souad thanks God that her grandfather will not go to Hell because she does not want any of her relatives to burn in Hell.

Her mother continues to wear black for 40 days. She also turns off the radio, and Souad no longer hears her laugh in that loud voice that used to reach her ears even when she was in the field. But after 40 days, everything returns to what it used to be. Her mother stops wearing black and her laughter starts to ring in the house.

Her mother has a loud, distinctive laugh. She hears it when she is in the street and her heart becomes joyful and she feels safe. As long as her mother laughs, it means she is alive and her father is still alive and everything in their house is as it used to be.

A deeply buried feeling has accompanied her since childhood that, some time, she will not find her mother, or that her father will suddenly die or disappear and she will have no shelter, no one to take care of her, feed her, or pay her expenses.

As much as she fears that her father might die, she also imagines that it is death only that could free her from studying and from school.

There is no secondary school for girls in Desouk. Souad is happy and thinks that she will not be going to school; but her mother suggests she join the Al-Abbasiya Secondary School for girls and live in her deceased grandfather's house.

Her grandfather's house is still sealed in Souad's memory with a dark cloud of hatred. She does not love her grandfather, and her grandfather is no longer in the house because he died. But she also doesn't like her aunt. She neither loves nor hates her grandmother, and her uncle is like her grandfather, although she loves him more.

More important than this is that she will be living in Al-Abbasiya, away from Desouk and away from her father. A strong sense of joy stirs her heart secretly for the mere fact that she will live in a house that doesn't have her father in it.

* * *

The last night before she leaves Desouk, her mother comes and lies down beside her in her bed. She pats her back with her white plump hand as she used to do when she was a child. Her soft voice whispers in her ear:

You will be responsible for yourself, Souad, in your grandfather's house. You have to study without anyone prompting you; you have grown up and you don't need anyone to tell you what is in your interest. Your interest, my daughter, is at school and in education. Education raises a human being to the highest position, and I used to love education when I was like you. I wished to learn everything: English, French, playing the piano, and horse-riding. But your late grandfather was a tough man. He used to educate a girl until the age of 15 then take her out of school and make her stay at home until a bridegroom came for her. I cried when he took me out of school. I used to hate the house and couldn't stand to live in it, especially when my father was in the house. He never used to stop quarreling with my mother, and when he went out I would be happy. When he returned, I would go into my room and not come out. I used to pray that I would marry anyone and leave that house. I was 16 when your father came to ask for my hand. My sister

Dawlat used to make fun of me and tell me that the bridegroom is a peasant and his family members are peasants. I told her: Peasant or no peasant, I am content with anyone for the sake of leaving your house and leaving everyone in it. On the day of the engagement I looked from behind the shutter in order to see the face of the man I was going to marry. I only saw his back, because he sat with his back to the shutter. I told myself what is important is to get married and get out of this house, and it isn't important that I see him. They had the engagement then the wedding. We got married and the first residence we had was in Kobri El Obba, the apartment I gave birth to you in. The minute I got married I became pregnant with you. Your grandmother the Hajja saw me pregnant and said to me: You are carrying a boy, Nihad. I asked her: How do you know, Mother-in-law? She told me: I know who is bearing a boy from the radiance of her eyes and who bears a girl from the yellowness of her face. I used to laugh and tell her: Shame on you, Hajja, a girl is like a boy. Your grandmother would get angry and say: A boy is worth ten girls. I used to say: On the contrary, the girl is better than a boy and I pray God to give me a girl.

Souad closes her eyes and sleeps and thanks God that he listened to her mother's prayer and made her a girl and not a boy. She imagines that she might have been a boy if it weren't for her mother's prayer. She thanks God once more who made her mother remember such a prayer when she was pregnant. She could have forgotten, because she forgets many things and always forgets where she placed the cupboard key.

Her mind wonders as she sleeps how the fate of boys or girls is determined by such coincidences, just because the mother remembered the prayer or forgot it. She tells herself:

But if my mother forgets to pray and the result is that she gave birth to me as a boy would I be responsible for this mistake or would my mother be responsible? And who is responsible, my mother or God, because it is God who accepts a prayer or rejects it. He is the one who creates people and decides their fate and their organs whether boys or girls.

In the morning, her father carries her suitcase for her and waves to her mother as she looks at them from the window. She smiles at him, but her eyes shine as if they are crying. Souad feels heavy-hearted and wants to turn around and go to her mother to embrace her and kiss her. She actually turns around and sees her mother's face from far away like a small, round patch of light shining by the window. She stops walking. Her father looks at her and says:

Quick or the train will leave.

On the train, the movement of the lampposts does not bring her joy as they move backwards and the train's rapid movement does not make her happy. She feels that the train is carrying her far away from her mother at a crazy speed, and she loves her mother in spite of everything and in spite of the fact that her mother obeys her father blindly and sides with him against her. But she feels that her mother loves her and was so sad to part from her, so she cried. She, too, is sad to part from her mother, but she does not cry like her, and she should not cry no matter what happens. She has grown up and no longer cries as she used to when she was a child. Her heart was young and got affected quickly and hurt quickly. But now, her heart has matured and solidified and nothing hurts her.

She swallows her tears as she sits next to her father on the train. Her father remains silent until they reach her grandfather's house in Al-Abbasiya. She sees her grandmother sitting in the hall in her black dress. She parts her lips when she sees her and says in a soft voice:

Welcome.

Her father answers and the silence resumes once more. Her aunt comes wearing black and says in a low, sad voice:

Welcome.

Her father answers and the silence resumes once more in the big hall.

After her father drinks his coffee, he says that he will be returning to Desouk and her grandmother says in a soft voice:

Why don't you spend the night here and leave in the morning?

Her father says that he has work in the morning and that he has to travel back the same day. Her grandmother rises and shakes his hand and her aunt shakes hands with him, too. Her father approaches her and reaches out his hand saying:

I'm returning to Desouk, Souad, and I am leaving you here in the care of your grandmother and aunt. I want to hear from them only good news about you, that you are studying your lessons and not wasting your time.

Her father continues to hold her hand and almost hugs her but refrains. A small muscle twitches below his nose, and she realizes from her father's eyes that he is suppressing deep inside himself something that resembles love. He seems to really love her but is embarrassed to show this love to himself or to others.

He lets go of her hand and turns toward the door. She sees his back slightly bent, which is something she has never noticed before. She almost runs after him and says:

Don't leave me.

But she is embarrassed because she is no longer a child, and everyone who sees her says that she has grown up and has become a big girl.

Her eyes remain fixed on his back until he descends the stairs and goes out of the garden gate. Her father turns back before he disappears, and he waves. She raises her hand and waves

back with a heavy heart, then turns and goes
inside the hall where she sees her grandmother
sitting. She remains standing beside her, not
knowing what to do until she hears her faint voice
say to her:

> *Come, Souad, sit beside me. Why are you standing
> like that?*

Before she sleeps that night, her grandmother
sits beside her and talks to her about the days of
the past. She tells her that her grandfather was a
wealthy man and had a big country estate. The
Khedive Ismail was a close friend of his, but this
friendship brought them poverty. The Khedive
was a spendthrift and corrupt, to the point of
becoming bankrupt and having to borrow from
his wealthy friends. One of them was your grandfather, who sold his estate and lent the Khedive all
its price. The only thing he took from this was a
small piece of paper like a receipt. The only thing
they inherited from her father was this receipt,
which they kept locked in a drawer in the hope
that they will get it out one day and ask for their
right.

Souad learns from her grandmother that the
receipt is still in one of the drawers in the house of
one of the men in her family, and that she still has
hope of getting back the estate. She believes that
God is just and that He will never let the right of
one of his servants go. She believes that she will
inherit her portion of the estate, and that after she

dies Souad's mother will inherit her full portion. Her grandmother sighs as she says to her:

After a long time and after your mother has her fill of this world, you will inherit your portion when she dies, Souad.

Souad is 11 years old and she has heard this story before from her mother. She feels some sort of pride and joy because she belongs to a rich family of this sort. She told her friends at school the story and how the Khedive borrowed her ancestors' money, which means that they were richer than the Khedive. She found out from history that the Khedive was the king's grandfather and she felt prouder. She imagined that she was at the same level as the king, or maybe better than him because the king's grandfather borrowed money from her grandfather but her grandfather did not borrow money from anyone.

The walls of her grandfather's house are covered with pictures. She recognizes the Khedive in one of them because it resembles his picture in the history book. She becomes certain when she sees the picture that the Khedive did, in fact, take the money from the estate and that he was a family friend, or else why would they hang his picture in the house? Among the pictures she also sees the portrait of Saad Zaghloul. She tells this to her friends at school because she feels some sort of pride.

She always searches for stories to tell her friends to feel that she is better than them. She feels inferior to them and that they are brighter than her and more able to learn their lessons. All these stories about her grandfathers and the glories of her family achieve nothing, and her feeling of being less than the others remains suppressed deeply in her chest and hurts her. The thing that pains her most is that she is inferior to her brother Mustafa. She has heard her mother say many times that Mustafa is very intelligent. Her father always says that Mustafa has inherited his intelligence because he is always first in his class.

Her father never directly says that Mustafa is more intelligent than her, but she feels from the way he looks at them that he is comparing her with her brother and admiring him rather than her. His admiration for her brother only indicates that he did not admire her. She suppresses the bitterness and pain inside herself and pretends not to know the meaning of her father's looks; she sometimes joins her father in admiring her brother's intelligence and expressing happiness because of this. In reality, she does not feel any joy, and joining her father in praising her brother seems to her like a confession that her brother is better than her. It is a confession she does not express, but it makes her feel doubly humiliated, as if she were joining her father in not admiring herself. She feels suffocated, but she lies to please her father and agrees with his opinion, even if this opinion is against her own self. Her self becomes something she despises because she cannot defend it and express her true opinion.

Her true opinion is that she does not love her brother, and whenever her mother's and father's admiration of him increases, she hates him more. She sees a look in her brother's eyes that she does not like. He is supposed to be 4 years younger than her, but he does not treat her like an elder sister. An elder sister is a respectable title that helps make up for her feeling of inferiority. She repeats in front of him all the time that she is the elder sister and the elder sister warrants respect. But Mustafa is not afraid of her, and he fixes his gaze on her as if he is defying her. Her blood boils in her veins with anger and she beats him. As she beats him, she feels that he is stronger than her and physically superior, which increases her inner feeling that she is less worthy than him.

Souad gets attached to her grandmother because her grandmother expresses all the time, in the spacious hall where she sits, her admiration of her and how she does not admire her Uncle Hassanein. She says that he is a reckless young man who wastes his money by going to the cinema and going out with girls. She does not know at first why her grandmother admires her, but she tells her that she admires her because she prays regularly but her Uncle Hassanein does not pray, fast, or know God, and he has inherited these manners from his late father, and God will punish him and will not make him successful because he disobeys her. Her grandmother tells her that she has inherited her mother's looks and not those of her Uncle Hassanein, praise be to God. She warns her against imitating her uncle or sitting with him in the same room when his girlfriends come over. Her mother and father also warn her. Her father advises her to lock her room and study, and not to waste time by going to the cinema because the cinema corrupts and God has forbidden corruption and has forbidden the relationship between a man and a woman except after marriage.

Souad used to listen to her father's words and believe and obey him without any effort or thought. It is her father who knows her best interest and she does not know her own interest as her father always says. He is the one who takes care of her expenses and she cannot live without a father who supports her or without a home and family. Life is big and evil people are many, and the night is dark and full of thieves and murderers. Al-Abbasiya is a huge city, unlike Desouk. She knows nothing of its many streets except the way from the house to school. When she walks in the street alone, she feels that she is a stranger; no one knows her and she knows no one. She is afraid of going out on her own at night and wants the Eid break to come soon so she can see her mother, father, sister, and brother. She starts to love them all, and they love her and write her letters in which they say that they miss seeing her. In Al-Abbasiya, no one misses her in the house or at school. Its streets are strange and unknown and full of unfamiliar faces, among whom there must be thieves and burglars. It is also full of corruption from the cinema, men, alcohol, and funfairs. Her father and God and her mother and grandmother have all forbidden it. She has no choice but to close the door of her room and study and pray regularly so that God will protect her from any harm as her father advised her.

She starts to love long holidays because she can go to Desouk. The summer holiday is the longest and she loves it the most. The big Eid break is better than the small Eid break, because it is longer, and watching the butcher as he slaughters the sheep every Eid is a greater pleasure than watching her mother bake cookies before the small Eid. Also, the Eid prayer moves her heart and her ears wake up to that particular prayer at dawn during Eid and the voice of thousands calling out in one voice:

Allah is greater … manifold praises to Allah … glory to Allah by morning and night…

Also, her father reaches out with the Eid pocket money, which is more pocket money than any other day. She wears a new pair of shoes and a new dress and goes out into the street proud among the neighbors' boys and girls and buys with all her pocket money wind pipes, bombs, and colored balloons.

But the thing that excites her the most is that moment when the butcher strikes the sheep's neck and blood rushes out like a fountain on the bathroom floor as the four limbs jerk and violently contract, and the wide open eyes of the sheep look at her in pain, sorrow, and rebuke as if it is asking her:

Why didn't you tell me that they will slaughter me as you fed me clover? Were you conspiring with them against me while you patted my back?

Happiness disappears from Souad's heart and she feels heavy, and the joy of Eid disappears, and the sheep's meat that her mother is frying in ghee feels heavy in her stomach. She eats it without joy and she imagines the sheep's eyes as she eats, looking at her in sorrow and wondering:

Why are they slaughtering me?

She does not know the answer to this question, so she asks her father. Her father tells her the story of Prophet Abraham, who was one day surprised by a strange message from God that he had to obey immediately without asking or discussing. God's orders are to be obeyed and not discussed, and a human doesn't have to know their reasons or their wisdom. God has his own wisdom that is above a human's brain. The order that Prophet Abraham received was to slaughter his son Isaac with a knife on top of the mountain, and Abraham took his son to the mountain to slaughter him.

Souad's joints shake as she listens to her father and imagines the small son climbing the mountain beside his father and feeling his neck in terror, and he does not know why his father is slaughtering him, although he has not made a mistake and not committed any sin to provoke God's anger. Souad asks in a quivering voice:

Why is God punishing Isaac by slaughtering him when he never committed any sin?

Her father says:

God was not punishing Isaac but was testing his father Abraham with this difficult task, to see if he will obey God's order or not. Prophet Abraham passed the test and obeyed God. He placed the knife on his son's neck to slaughter him ... (Souad's heart beats faster and her breath becomes shorter as she feels her neck with shaking fingers) ... *and in the final minute before the knife slit the son's throat, as God became certain of Abraham's obedience, God brought down a sheep from heaven for Abraham to slaughter instead of his son as a reward for obeying God. For obedience, my daughter, is the greatest of virtues.*

Souad was still shaking and her mind was preoccupied with the small son who presented his throat for slaughtering and who must have died from terror when the knife came close to his neck. But no one thought of the son's psychological state; even God Himself did not care except for testing the father's obedience on behalf of the son. The father did not hesitate in showing this obedience and he passed the test. As for the son, what happened to him after this terrifying experience? If the father had hesitated and failed the test, then would the son have been slaughtered because his father was disobedient? How can God be content with punishing the son because of the father's sin? Is this justice?

She pants and her lips part as she is about to ask her father, but she does not. Her father has trained her for many years not to ask and not to think too much about God's plan. But her mind is thinking despite her will, and her heart beats fast despite her desire. A kind of terror creeps over her body and neck, and her eyes look stealthily at her father. She tries to examine her father's features and figure out whether he would slaughter her if God ordered him to or not. Why does God give parents such frightful tasks for their children, and why doesn't God think of the children's feelings?

She no longer asks herself many old questions from childhood. She realizes that questioning is forbidden and such thinking is a form of disbelieving in God and in God's justice. God is just whether He is fair, unjust, or oppressive, and God is merciful whether He slaughters children or does not slaughter them.

In her grandfather's big house, she no longer has these childish thoughts and her mind becomes preoccupied with many studies, for secondary school is more difficult than primary, the books are bigger and the exams are more difficult. The minute she returns from school, she sits in her room and studies until night time. Night in her grandfather's silent big house is scary, and her grandfather's spirit might come out any night in the form of a ghost. A ghost is like a jinn, and it knows what a human does not know. Her grandfather's ghost might know that she did not love him, so he will attack her one of those nights, just to retaliate.

Because of the extent of her fear, she sits beside her grandmother whether she is in the hall or in her room. She sometimes follows her to the bathroom and waits for her in front of the door until she comes out. Her grandmother's appearance does not give her much relief. Her head is covered

in black and her body is all in black. Only a face
with strange features appears, with gray eyes that
may see her or not. Her tight lips do not indicate
whether she is silent, speaking, breathing, or has
stopped breathing. When silence pervades the
house, she sharpens her ears to hear her breath
or to watch her chest rise and fall. She fears that
everything in her might stop suddenly and she,
too, will die, just like her grandfather. She does
not want her to die until after she graduates from
secondary school, because she is the only one who
entertains her in this house. She does not entertain
her with words, as she is silent most of the time,
but the sound of her breath erases her fears of her
grandfather's ghost. Also, if she dies, too, then
there will be two ghosts instead of one ghost in the
house.

*　*　*

In the library of the secondary school she finds
many books filled with love stories. The word *love*
used to frighten her, and she would close the book
and stop reading. She would perform her ablution
and pray and ask God to forgive her sin.

She feels some relief after prayer, as if God has
accepted her repentance and forgiven her sin and
returned her to His grace with the holy ones.
But she goes to the library once more to read
and feels pleasure as she reads books and stories.
But the pleasure is accompanied by fear of God's
punishment and burning in Hell, so she rushes to
perform her ablution and pray and repent.

Reading with pleasure, fright, and pain repeats itself, followed by a stronger feeling of sin and a sense of humiliation, weakness, corruption, and fear of God's punishment. Her father's voice comes to her as she sleeps and tells her in anger:

You have to expel the devil from your mind and spirit.

She closes her eyes and tries to sleep and expel the devil that drives her to read books outside the school curriculum.

The lessons that the male and female teachers teach her are dull and devoid of meaning. They are disconnected and nothing unites them. She is unable to understand a thing and she must simply learn the lessons by heart as if she is memorizing the Koran.

At the end of the year, she passes the exam with distinction and returns to Desouk to spend the summer vacation with her father, mother, sister, and brother. She is 11 years of age and has become tall. Two small buds have sprouted on her chest, each the size of a grape or an olive.

Her grandmother and aunts visit them during the holiday, and she hears whispers behind her. She does not quite know what has taken place. When the new school year begins, her father does not ask her to prepare her bag, and they start to call her *the bride*. A man with a strange appearance comes and they called him *the bridegroom*. One noisy and crowded night, with drums beating, they make her walk beside this man with her hand in his. She wears a white dress and her face is as white as the dress.

The door closes behind her alone with this man. She is a child of eleven and a half years and when the door opens in the morning, she is no longer Souad the child. In one night she has leaped from childhood to old age, and then she dies after she gives birth to a child who resembles her, whom she calls Souad.

CHAPTER 4

Nawal El Saadawi and a History of Oppression: Brief Biographical Facts

- Born on October 27, 1931 in the small village of Kafr Tahla to a father who was a government official in the Ministry of Education and a mother who was a housewife and made to stay at home at the age of 15 and not finish her education.

- In 1941, Abdel Maksoud Effendi asked for her hand in marriage and she tipped the coffee tray all over his chest. Otherwise, she would have ended up married at an early age like Souad.

- In 1955, she graduated as a medical doctor from Cairo University.

- She married a fellow student in medical school, Ahmed Helmy, who was engaged in fighting

© Omnia Amin 2016, Published by Palgrave Macmillan,   153
A Division of Nature America Inc.
N. El Saadawi, *Diary of a Child Called Souad*,
DOI 10.1007/978-1-137-58730-5

against the British, but they divorced as he became embittered and turned to drugs. They have a daughter, Mona Helmy, who became a doctor in economics and a writer, poet, and activist like her mother. She has her own column in *Tahrir Daily* in Cairo and writes about creativity and daring topics that, on one occasion, led her to court accused of heresy.

- She later married a well-to-do lawyer. They quickly divorced because he forced her to choose between her marriage and her writing.

- In 1957, she published her first book, a collection of short stories called *I learnt Love*.

- In 1958, her mother died. One year later, her father passed away.

- In 1964, she married Dr. Sherif Hetata, a medical doctor and writer who was imprisoned for 13 years due to his political views. He also translated most of her works into English and became her lifelong husband and companion until they divorced in 2010. They have one son, Atef Hetata, who is a film director who chooses challenging themes and social problems to tackle.

- She studied at Columbia University, New York, and received her Master of Public Health degree in 1966.

- In 1969, she published her first nonfiction work, *Women and Sex*, in which she exposed the crimes committed against women's bodies, including circumcision.

- Held the position of Author for the Supreme Council for Arts and Social Sciences, Cairo.

- Became Director General of the Health Education Department, Ministry of Health, Cairo.

- Became Secretary General of Medical Association, Cairo.

- Worked as a Medical Doctor at the University Hospital and Ministry of Health. She lost her position in 1972 because of her writing and activism.

- Founded the Health Education Association.

- Founded the Egyptian Women Writers Association.

- Founded and became Chief Editor of *Health Magazine* in Cairo. After 3 years, in 1973, the magazine was closed down because of her activism and writing.

- Became editor of the *Medical Association Magazine*.

- From 1973 to 1976, she researched women and neurosis in the Ain Shams University's Faculty of Medicine, which inspired her to write one of her most famous novels of all, *Woman At Point Zero*.

- From 1979 to 1980, she was the UN Advisor for the Women's Programme in Africa (ECA) and Middle East (ECWA).

- In 1981, she helped publish a feminist magazine, *Confrontation* and, as a result, coupled with her political activism and writings, she was imprisoned by President Anwar El Sadat in Al Qanater Women's prison and was only released after his death.

- In 1982, she became the founder and president of the Arab Women Solidarity Association (AWASA), which is the first legal, independent feminist organization in Egypt and has more than 2000 members worldwide.

- In 1988, she was forced to flee Egypt because her name appears on an Islamic Fundamentalists' death list. She went to the United States to teach at Duke University's Asian and African Languages Department in North Carolina as well as the University of Washington in Seattle. She returned to Egypt in 1996.

- Co-founder of the Arab Association for Human Rights.

- In 1991, AWASA's magazine *Noon* is closed down by the government, of which she was editor-in-chief. Six months later, AWASA was declared illegal after criticizing US involvement in the Gulf War.

- In 2001, three of her books were banned at the Cairo International Book Fair.

- In 2002, a court case was brought against her by a lawyer who sought to have her forcibly divorced from her husband on the basis of apostasy (abandonment of religion).

- In 2004, she won the North-South prize from the Council of Europe.

- Since her book *The Fall of the Imam* was published in 1987, she started receiving death threats from fundamentalist religious groups. The book was finally banned in 2004.

- In 2005, she won the Inana International Prize in Belgium.

- She ran in the Egyptian presidential election in 2005.

- In 2005, her book *The Novel* was banned.

- In 2006, her play *God Resign at the Summit* was banned in Egypt. She faced a new trial against her raised by Al Azhar, who accused her of apostasy and heresy because of that play. She won the case in 2008.

- On January 28, 2007, she was accused, along with her daughter Mona Helmy, of apostasy and interrogated by the General Prosecutor in Cairo for wanting to honor the name of the mother. They won the case and, as a result, every child born outside marriage in Egypt was given the right to carry the name of the mother.

- In 2008, her efforts for more than 50 years to ban female genital mutilation (FGM) were rewarded as FGM was banned in Egypt.

- In 2007, she receives two honorary doctorates in Belgium from Vrije Universiteit Brussel and from the Université Libre de Belgique.

- In 2011, she participated with the protesters in Tahrir Square during the Egyptian demonstrations in Cairo.

- In 2012, she received the Stig Dagerman Award in Sweden.

- She is the author of more than 50 works of fiction and nonfiction that have been translated into more than 40 languages. Some of them are taught in a number of universities all over the world.

CHAPTER 5

Interview with Nawal El Saadawi[1]

Conducted by Omnia Amin

Was *Diary of a Child Called Souad* your first major attempt at writing?

Diary of a Child Called Souad was not my first attempt at writing, but it was the only one that survived destruction and burning, which happened to my other childhood diaries. Since I learned how to write I had kept a secret diary, which I burned or destroyed. I was afraid that somebody might find it.

Do you consider *Diary of a Child Called Souad* a work of fiction or nonfiction?

Diary of a Child Called Souad reflects my feelings when I was 12 and 13 years of age. It is fiction

[1] Interview with Dr. Nawal El Saadawi originally conducted in Arabic and translated into English by Dr. Omnia Amin, December 1, 2012.

© Omnia Amin 2016, Published by Palgrave Macmillan,   159
A Division of Nature America Inc.
N. El Saadawi, *Diary of a Child Called Souad*,
DOI 10.1007/978-1-137-58730-5

and nonfiction together—like other memoirs. It is based on facts and events that happened in my childhood, but to write these events on paper as words means that you enter the world of symbols, language, which is fiction. I think facts and fiction are inseparable in writing.

Your first published work of fiction is a collection of short stories entitled *I Learned Love*, published in 1957, while your first piece of nonfiction, *Woman and Sex*, was published almost a decade later in 1969. Do you think it was your private life that prompted you to become a writer more than your public role as a physician and an activist for human rights?

During the 1940s and 1950s I was writing poems, short stories, articles, and memoirs. Many of them were destroyed or lost; others survived. I was able to publish a collection of my short stories in a book in 1957. Some of my articles which I collected and published in *Woman and Sex* were written during the 1950s when I was a medical student. At that time, I could not publish except in university magazines or other small journals.

I cannot say that my private life prompted me to write more than my public life. I cannot separate between private and public in reality.

***I Learned Love* was published 1 year before your mother died. How did your mother and your**

family receive your writing? Did you encounter any form of resistance and restriction from your family in your later writing and publication?

My mother and father encouraged me to write poems and short stories. In fact, it was my mother who played a big role in the survival of *Diary of a Child Called Souad*, and my father, too. Both loved literature and imagination. Both were happy when my first collection of short stories *I Learned Love* was published as a book. They read many of these stories in magazines or journals before they were collected in the book. They were proud of my literary work. They were critical of the regime like me. They wanted to protect me, of course, from any harm, but they never stopped me from writing. They died in 1958 and 1959, before I started to be more radical and more critical in my fiction and nonfiction.

You once stated in an interview that children criticize God and religion because they have common sense. Souad asks many questions and silently uncovers hypocrisy in her culture. Did you hold this belief in mind when you were writing *Diary of A Child Called Souad*?

Yes, I was sensitive from childhood to paradoxes and contradiction in the life around me, at home, in the street, in school, on the radio, in books we read in school, including the Bible and Koran. I remember that other children in the family and my schoolmates shared my feelings about the hypocrisy everywhere around us, but we were not aware yet of why such hypocrisy exists in culture or religion or politics or other areas.

Your female characters always appear stronger and more admirable than the men. You once said that literature has to serve society: is this why you depict strong female characters, as part of empowering women? Have there been strong men who have influenced your life and your writing?

I met few strong men and women in my life who I admired. I wrote about some of them that inspired me to write about them. But it is normal for a man to be strong, as this is regarded as part of manhood. Normal people do not inspire me much. It is abnormal for a woman to be herself and be strong also. Such characters are more inspiring than others. I write about them because they inspire me, not as part of empowering women.

You insisted on the act of writing even when you were in prison, and you associate it with dissidence. You also associate true creativity with dissidence. In your earliest writings we see how Souad is plagued with dissident thoughts she never has the courage to pursue. Can you

elaborate on the importance of dissidence in terms of writing and creativity?

I teach creativity and dissidence; this is my interest, to look at the relation between creativity and dissidence—and revolution. Collective dissidence leads to revolution. When the law is unjust you have to break it; this is dissidence. When the system is unjust you have to change it; this is revolution. When you are creative, you are sensitive to injustice and hypocrisy; you never lose the ability of children to be themselves and speak the truth.

We lose our creative power in the early years of life because of bad education and oppression and strong political–religious taboos. I do not teach creativity to my students, but what I do is to undo what education did to them, and how oppression and fear stifled their creativity.

You said that in your 30s you did not have the courage to write about many painful and sensitive issues in your life, and it took you another 30 years to be able to do so. With which particular book did you start writing about inhibited areas in your life, and was there a particular incident that prompted you to do this?

There is no particular incident in my life that liberated me from my inhibitions. Liberation from deep embedded historical inhibitions is a gradual, progressive process that happens all our life from birth to death. This thread of liberation may be cut or may be strengthened by certain incidents in childhood or adulthood. I was lucky to have my parents, who did not cut this thread in my childhood. I was lucky also in my adulthood to fight wrong husbands and bad political regimes. The struggle against oppression can build our immunity and strengthen our creativity and dissidence.

Your life has been one big struggle after another. If your life had been different, do you think you would still have become the Nawal El Saadawi of today?

Yes, my life has been one struggle after another. Like a horse jumping one obstacle after another: the higher the obstacle, the higher the challenge. If my life had been different, if I had had an easy life with no challenges ... I do not know, maybe I would have not become what I am, or maybe I would have become the same person but with a different personality and goals in life.

If you had your life to live all over again, what would you change?

If I had my life to live all over again I would change nothing except giving more time to swimming and music.

You have extremely successful children. Is this due to the different kind of upbringing they had? What advice would you give to young readers of Souad's age, and to parents?

My daughter and son are creative and dissident in their own ways. They enjoyed freedom and independence in childhood. They led their own struggles in adulthood and participated in the revolutions against the oppressive political system in Egypt. Parents should leave their children to grow naturally and creatively without their interference. They should not frighten their children with hellfire or God's punishment, or any other punishment. Fear destroys natural creativity in children. Parents should encourage their children to be critical. The creative mind is critical, dissident, not obedient.

INDEX

© Omnia Amin 2016, Published by Palgrave Macmillan, 167
A Division of Nature America Inc.
N. El Saadawi, *Diary of a Child Called Souad*,
DOI 10.1057/978-1-137-58730-5

Printed by Books on Demand, Germany